PLAY IT FORWARD

Visit us at www.boldstrokesbooks.com

PLAY IT FORWARD

by

Frederick Smith

A Division of Bold Strokes Books

2015

PLAY IT FORWARD

ISBN 13: 978-1-62639-235-9

THIS TRADE PAPERBACK ORIGINAL IS PUBLISHED BY
BOLD STROKES BOOKS, INC.
P.O. BOX 249
VALLEY FALLS, NY 12185

FIRST EDITION: JANUARY 2015

CREDITS
EDITORS: GREG HERREN AND STACIA SEAMAN
PRODUCTION DESIGN: STACIA SEAMAN
COVER DESIGN BY GABRIELLE PENDERGRAST

PREFACE

Our communities have made lots of progressive history in the past few years or so. A lot has changed since 2009, the year this novel is set:

- The election of President Barack Obama, Michelle Obama, and a Black First Family in the White House.
- Marriage equality bans being challenged and struck down by state and federal courts.
- Revenge porn laws, making it a prosecutable crime to "get back" at someone online if they choose to leave a relationship.
- Sports heroes like Jason Collins and Michael Sam, among others, declaring who they are and making it easier to be out, proud, and a current professional in sports.
- Talented musicians like Frank Ocean, among others, declaring who he is and making it easier to be out, proud, and a current professional in hip-hop, R&B, and pop music.

The public figures make it easy.

The private figures, those neighborhood celebrities, so to speak, do the hard work in Black, Chicana/o Latina/o, Asian Pacific Islander communities to make life easier for their community members to accept their same-gender-loving, two-spirit, gay, queer family members and friends. They run community organizations in their own 'hoods to make life easier…to be a safer space…to show the intersections of race, class, and gender.

My hat goes off to the professionals who run these LGBTQ organizations in their communities and on college campuses. My hat goes off to my Student Affairs and Student Union colleagues who work to help all students—but especially queer students and queer students of color—find a home away from home. My hat goes off to the scholars doing people of color, queer, and queer people of color scholarship on their campuses, making sure that these stories are given their proper place in academia and history. There are too many to be named, but if you know them…applaud them. If you are one…pat yourself on the back.

A lot has happened since the 2008 election of President Barack Obama. We've made history. We have a lot more work to do—challenging racism, classism, sexism within the LGB community. Helping to push forward an agenda for the transgender community. Seeing connections between all oppressions, and not just the ones that directly affect you.

You can do a lot more to make history, wherever and whoever you are.

Yes, we can all make change!

Frederick Smith
September 2014

CHAPTER 1

June 2009

Much of the trouble started when that video I made, but didn't *really* make, hit the Internet.

I was on my second round of Grey Goose and tonics with my best friend Kyle and his longtime love, Bernard. It was a seventy-degree Sunday evening in June, just before the large rush of *younger* Black guys made their way into The Abbey in West Hollywood, just before the ambient lounge music transitioned to the current hip-hop songs. Though we enjoyed a good time out, we enjoyed it with the company of other thirty-somethings, and at a time of day when we could actually hear our conversations above the sound of music.

Kyle, Bernard, and I were this close to winding down our time together—as we all worked and had somewhere to be on Monday morning—when Bernard, troublemaker that he is, brought up the long-gone Clinton-Obama rift of 2008. He knew how to get me started and thus delay our departure.

"I still can't believe you voted for that lady, Malcolm," Bernard said rather loudly, his cocktail swirling but never spilling out of the glass in his left hand. "I am still holding that against you. You lost your Black card with me."

"Oh gosh," Kyle said and rolled his eyes. Everyone knew Bernard loved a debate…and trouble. Kyle could be equally dramatic. That made them a good match for the past eight years. "Here we go again. That was almost a year ago. Give it a rest."

"No worries," I said. "I'm not going to get into it. We all know Hillary was much more experienced and ready for day one on the job than Barack was."

Bernard rolled his eyes and continued, "How can you say that? Most of her alleged experience was on her husband's watch."

That was when I noticed my phone ringing. A call from my sister in Indiana. A downer, much like the political debate Bernard was trying to reel me into again. I wasn't feeling having this political commentary over cocktails, especially for an election competition a year behind us.

"Having that inside knowledge of how things work and how to make things happen *is* experience," I said. "It's called social and cultural capital, but it's all a moot point. Election is long over. We made history and Barack is the man."

"True, but I'm a long way from forgetting," Bernard said with a laugh. Raised his glass to mine and we toasted. Political rivals in our minds, but friends because he loved my best friend Kyle. "To unity…and change."

"Yeah, whatever," I said reluctantly, and toasted with Bernard and Kyle. Noticed a lot of our thirty-something acquaintances were being replaced by twenty-somethings. That tended to happen just around seven on Sunday evenings at The Abbey. "The kids are starting to arrive, and I want to be gone before it gets too crowded and all that drama that comes with them starts. And I definitely don't want to see anyone from LADS."

"Amen to that, girl," Kyle said and placed his almost-empty glass on a nearby table. "I don't know how these kids stay out all night on Sunday, as if they don't have to work or go to school on Monday. I'm already going over my to-do list in my mind."

"Please, baby," Bernard interrupted. "Most of them don't have jobs. Trifling little things. So glad I'm not on the market now."

Bernard kissed Kyle on the cheek, and they gave each other that look lovers give when they want to do couples things in bed later. I felt like quite the third wheel, though it's something Kyle and Bernard would never say out loud. We'd been doing our Sunday afternoon meetings at The Abbey for years, even before Black people started taking over Sundays.

"I don't know how they can afford these fifteen-dollar drinks like they do," I said. The Abbey was known for its pricey mojitos and martinis of all flavors, but most people ignored the prices, as the bar was the best place to see and be seen in gay and gay-friendly L.A. We were all playing Hollywood, even if it wasn't our reality. I'd exchanged my standard khaki pants and button-down for something a little more casual and Abbey-worthy. Hollywood, I could never quite fit the part or find myself paying for those designers and labels that many wore...just because. I'd never been the fit-in-just-because type.

"Okaaaay."

"Most of them are pretending to be someone's stylist, assistant, or an actor, or whatever," I said. "You wouldn't believe how many 'models' and 'singers' come into LADS for the free food vouchers...Oh, okay, go ahead and make out while I talk, guys." I did air-quotes around the so-called careers of the young men I encountered in my day job.

Bernard whispered a sweet nothing in Kyle's ear and pulled him closer. Eight years and still happy. Still making out with each other like day one, they looked like two chocolate drops joined at the hip.

As my friends hugged and kissed each other, out of the corner of my eye I could see a group of young brothas, probably in their early twenties, staring and pointing our way. First, I thought it was the rare surprise of seeing Black-on-Black romance in West Hollywood that caught their curiosity and attention. Black guys were friends, not potential love interests, in West Hollywood. I was sure none of them had had any Black romantic couples as role models, but then again I couldn't assume anything these days. My work with young, Black gay men at the LADS organization opened my eyes to the fact that not everyone grew up middle class with two parents like I did. The job definitely challenged my upbringing and comfort zone. Nothing was a surprise. Anything could happen, and often did.

Much like it did when one of the twenty-something men, dressed in a black V-neck T-shirt, gray shorts, and black Oakland Raiders hat, nodded at me as a directive to walk his way. I excused myself from Kyle and Bernard, as they were on their way to third base and ignoring me at the moment, and walked across the room toward the massive fireplace near the front of The Abbey where brotha stood.

"Hey," I said.

Didn't know much else to say. His presence intimidated me a bit. Young, athletic, cute, masculine brotha. Definitely not the type that would put me in his target demographic. I knew he had to be a good ten years younger than me. But I wasn't looking for any type of romantic relationship, so shyness and intimidation wasn't necessary. As I got closer to him, I could tell he loved Hanae Mori cologne. Smelled good on him.

"Whaddup, bro?"

"Not much," I said.

He held out his free hand to fist-bump mine.

"What you up to?"

"Just about to head out," I said, deepening my voice, shortening my phrasing, performing masculinity. "Came in earlier with a couple buddies over there."

"Damn, thas too bad," he said and smiled. Nice set of pearly whites contrasted beautifully against his rich mahogany skin. "You looking good, bro."

"Thanks," I said, and replied like a nerd, "You don't look so bad yourself. I like your cologne."

This small talk on looking good was definitely a set-up for a one-nighter, since we hadn't even exchanged names yet. After a couple Grey Goose and tonics, I could have been game, had brotha not looked like some of the clients I served at LADS. I wasn't going to turn into one of those thirty-something midlife-crisis cases who got off on picking up guys who could be their younger brother, cousin, or worse yet, son. Back in my twenties and early thirties, when I was single and desperately looking for *anyone*, and working at the bank, I would have taken a guy like this home for the night. No questions asked. No background check. Sometimes no names exchanged. That was how I'd ended up with a string of exes whose lives were the social issue of the month. Now, I was happily single and looking for more than a one-night-only kind of arrangement. And I definitely wasn't looking for drama or to help someone else solve their drama. That was only for work.

"Turn around for me, man," he said. Snapped me back to reality from my dating flashback.

I smiled and said, "Excuse me?"

"I wanna see what you working with up close."

"You talking to the wrong guy," I said. "I'm not like that."

"Oh, so it's like that, then?" he said. "Thas okay, man. I seen your ass halfway across the room. I knew it was you. Thas whassup."

He nodded and pursed lips at me. Like he was sizing me up. I knew the look, having been around the block myself over the years. But I didn't know this young man, his history, health status, or motive for sizing me up.

"How about names?" I said, wanting to change the subject and get us on track to normal conversation. I'd pretty much determined I wasn't going to do anything with him beyond The Abbey. "I'm Malcolm. You're?"

"Just call me Compton for now," he said and nodded.

"As in…from Compton?" I said, a little confused, and waited for a response or explanation. None came. I'm such a nerd at times. Silence. "All right."

One of his friends brought back three drinks from the bar and handed two to Compton. Berry martinis in tall glasses.

"Take a sip," he said. "I want you all liquored up tonight, man. Thas whassup."

"Thanks," I said, to be polite. "But no thanks. I don't take drinks when I haven't seen them getting made. And I've already had two. Gotta drive."

"Two for me, then," he said. Chuckled. Tossed the straw out of one drink and gulped down about half in one swallow. "You one of them proper niggas, huh? That's cool. I know them proper niggas like you get freaky in the sheets."

I hated the whole tired conversation about who speaks like what. Kinda like how who voted for whom in primary elections a year ago validated one's membership in the Black community. I knew it—the talking-proper conversation—was a class thing, how people valued education as children, how people sized up community allegiance. But this was not the time for giving Compton a sociology lesson. Nor was I very keen on befriending a guy who, like many other young men without social skills, communicated his desires through sex talk and conquests.

"Compton, you don't know me and I don't know you," I said. "I understand you're young and probably don't know a lot about how real men want to be treated and approached, but the talk about sex. Not so much."

He put his berry martinis in an empty spot on the fireplace ledge and pulled out his iPhone.

"I know you well, Carlton," he said and ran his fingers across the face of the phone. Even though we were almost twenty years past *The Fresh Prince of Bel-Air* TV show, the character Carlton was still synonymous with being a proper-speaking Black nerd, even though I didn't think Carlton was a nerd.

My phone rang again. My sister, again, from Indianapolis. Must be urgent. No one calls long distance, over and over, without some kind of emergency. I knew something had to be up.

"It's Malcolm," I said, correcting Compton again. "Hold on a sec. I gotta take this. Be right back."

I walked toward the patio door at the front of The Abbey. Just a tad quieter than inside, but quiet enough for a thirty-something not to have to shout in the receiver of a cell phone.

"What's going on, Marlena?" I said. Don't laugh at my sister's name—our mom loved *Days of Our Lives* back in the day.

"It's your nephew, that's what's going on," she said. She sounded pissed off, once more, about Blake, her oldest son, my only nephew. Again, don't laugh at my nephew's name—my sister loved *Dynasty* as a teenager.

"What did Blake do now?"

"He's still spending all his goddamn time on that damn

Internet, meeting all kinds of strangers," Marlena said. "I just walked in on him getting head from this boy from down the street he went to high school with…and the house reeked of weed. I can't take it no more."

My sister Marlena had always had a difficult time with Blake. Her other kids, the twin girls, were angels compared to their older brother, born in Marlena's senior year of high school.

"So you're calling me for what?" I said. I mean, I knew she needed to vent. Who wouldn't, after catching their nineteen-year-old son getting a blow job from a neighbor.

"I'm tired of his Black ass…YOU HEAR ME, BLAKE, TIRED OF YOUR BLACK ASS…I SHOULD HAVE PUT HIM OUT A LONG TIME AGO," Marlena yelled to me, and I assume, to Blake, who'd probably slammed his bedroom door and wasn't paying attention to his mother. Why Marlena hadn't followed though on our family's "eighteen and out" rule was a mystery to me. We'd all known, including Marlena with her new baby back in the day, that it was expected we'd be out of the house after high school senior year, preferably at a college, but for sure working and in our own place.

"Hold on, Marlena," I said. "Let's talk about this."

It was my standard line to use with people who were having a dramatic moment. I knew hearing themselves out would help calm them down.

"Ain't nothing to talk about, Malcolm," Marlena said. "I can't put up with his trifling ass no more. I'm sending him out to California for the summer to stay with you, since he wants to be a rapper…AIN'T NO SUCH THING AS A GAY RAPPER, BLAKE."

"You're what?" I asked. I was sure I hadn't heard Marlena correctly. The "gay rapper" thing threw me off a bit.

"I *said* I'm sending him out to California for the summer,"

Marlena said. "What? You can't hear now, Malcolm? Trying to play LIKE YOU DON'T HEAR ME LIKE BLAKE DOES?"

"Calm down," I said. "Are you for real? Things that bad?" I asked.

"Yeah," she said. "You got a problem with it?"

Sunday evening, on a busy patio at The Abbey, wasn't the time to go through the list of reasons why having my nephew stay with me was a bad idea. So I started with just a few.

"Hel-LO," I said. "I'm working, busy all the time, running LADS, never home. And my place is so small. And what makes you think he'd want to spend his summer with his thirty-five-year-old uncle?"

And why would I want to spend my summer with a nineteen-year-old, when I see them every day at work? was what I really wanted to ask Marlena the dramatic.

"You work with the gays," she said. "Maybe you can straighten him out. I mean, not straighten him out like that, but help him get his life on track. If anybody can show him the way, I know you can. I'm done. I'M DONE!"

"Why can't he stay with Mama?" I asked.

"Mama's old," she said. "He'll get over on her quicker than me, and she'll just let her first grandbaby do whatever."

"Marlena," I said and sighed. "I'm far from perfect."

"Please?" Marlena said. "I'm tired. I'm sending him out there."

Compton walked out the patio door and toward me. With my sister putting me on the spot, and Compton looking kinda good in that black V-neck as he walked my way, I was ready to give Compton a one-night-only after The Abbey, or at minimum, a WeHo Hello in the parking structure around the corner. Sometimes, one-nighters aren't just about the sex. Sometimes they're a momentary denial to help get through life's realities.

"Whaddup, man? You coming back or what?"

"Okay," I said. And realized I'd answered both Marlena's and Compton's requests.

"Thanks, then we'll talk tomorrow," Marlena said, just as Compton replied, "Cool, see you inside."

"Wait," I said and realized I'd committed to both a summer with my nephew Blake and a continued conversation with Compton. Neither was of my own volition, but I knew it wouldn't hurt to give Blake or Compton a bit of my time.

I met Compton in the spot where I'd left him a few minutes earlier, in front of the fireplace. He'd finished the first drink his friend had given him and was well into the second. All in a matter of ten minutes or less. Mess.

"Anyway, Compton, I'm heading back to my buddies," I said. "Good meeting you. Have a good one."

"Wait," Compton said and wrapped his free arm around my waist while his hand drifted lower to my butt. "I wanna show you something, man. Look."

I removed his hand and moved a step away. "I know what you want to show me," I said. "Not interested."

He put the iPhone screen in my face, his arm around my shoulder. Squeezed. If I were planning to sleep with him, it would have felt...sexy. His touch was strong.

I saw the homepage of an amateur X-rated site uploading, and then two seconds later, I was doing something pornographic with my mouth to...

"Oh my God," I said. "Where did you get this?"

"It's on GayClick," Compton said and whispered/slurred in my ear, "You gone work my shit like that? I could use some bomb head."

"Hell no, I'm not working your sh…" I said. "What site is this? How did you get this video?"

"Hold on a sec," he said. "This is how I recognized yo ass across the room."

Two seconds later, I was onscreen doing something pornographic squatting up and down over...

"What the hell?" I said. "I've seen enough."

"Me too, but there's about six or seven more," he said and grinned. Slid a hand down to my butt and groped again. "You gone twerk that ass for me like you did in the video? Thas whassup, man."

"Are you crazy," I said and pulled away from Compton's grasp. "You don't even know me. That's not me." I knew it was me. But *how*...that was another question.

"You gone let me hit that, right?" Compton said. "Playin' all Carlton and shit, but fuck like a porn star."

"Fuck you," I said.

"I like it when you're hood like that," he said as I walked back to Kyle and Bernard. Watched Compton and his friends looking at the screen and getting a kick out of those videos with me in them. Videos I never EVER made.

"I gotta get out of here," I said. Felt like I was about to faint or vomit, but kept it together.

"Why? What's up?" Kyle said.

"What did that kid do to you?" Bernard asked. "I'll go fuck him up."

And I knew he would. Kyle too. But that wasn't what I wanted. Well, I did, but I also wanted to be able to return to The Abbey for future Sundays...years from now, after guys with iPhones with videos of me were no longer in the picture.

"I can't show my face in here again," I said. "I'm out."

I walked through the crowd, past Compton and his friends who jeered and whistled as I whisked by, and out the front entrance of The Abbey. I'm sure they all thought I was some kind of porn star or sexual acrobat. Maybe back in the day, pre-2000s, like before camera phones, sex tapes, paparazzi, and things that lived forever on computers, that kind of reputation might have been cool because it was all just based on word of mouth and not based on technology that could create a permanent marker of your reputation.

Not today. As a man in my thirties. With responsibilities. Role modeling. Clients. And a nineteen-year-old nephew coming to L.A. to spend the summer with me.

I looked for "him" in the long line of men waiting to get in the club. Not my nephew. But the one who sold me out online. Sometimes he would make an Abbey appearance on Sunday evenings, when he knew I'd probably be gone home and he wouldn't have to face me. He wasn't in line. No sign.

Meant one thing. He was at his place with the one he left me for.

And that was where I knew I'd be heading before I went home to my place.

CHAPTER 2

On the way to his house, my mind raced with a million messages I'd given to the young men at LADS.

At the Thursday night LADSrap group, three days earlier, I'd facilitated a talk I titled "Click This, Hit That: 2009," specifically on the issues and concerns that can come with an online presence and life, personal safety, and how the young men should exercise caution online if they ever aspired to do something beyond whatever they currently did to make ends meet.

"After all," I said and looked around the room at young Black men of all shades and sexual orientations, "Barack Obama never thought in a million years he'd be president. And he most certainly wouldn't have reached that goal if he'd ever sent or posted dirty pics of himself during his younger days on a computer or a cell phone."

Some of the guys snickered and laughed. A sign of guilt, I'm sure, that they'd already sent or seen plenty of inappropriate pictures on their technology and gadgets. Reality check. That was just what young people did.

"But he smoked out, didn't he? So your point is what, Mr. Malcolm? They didn't even have cell phones or computers back in those days." Question from the back of the circle from Sergio, a newcomer to LADS and LADSrap meetings.

"Because in case you didn't recognize, you're talking to us born in the late eighties to mid-nineties, and online is where it's at for our generation."

I loved and hated the pointed questions I got from the men who attended the groups. LADSrap was a new discussion group created by my front desk assistant, and personal pet project, DeMarco Jennings. It was designed as a way to engage young men in current events in a not-so-preachy way. DeMarco was great at the engagement part. I wasn't so great at the not-so-preachy part, but found ways to hold my tongue and make the weekly discussions a success.

"Sergio, keep it cute or put it on mute," DeMarco yelled from the side of the room, with a bit of a neck roll punctuating the end of his statement. I loved how he said the things I was thinking. "Let Malcolm finish. Go on, Malcolm."

"I keep it cute all the time," Sergio said and stood up. He pointed to his T-shirt, one of the many he designed and then sold on the streets after the various gay clubs in L.A., with one of his Sergio-isms, *No, I'm Not A Missed Connection...I Just Don't Like You.* "Thank you very much, DeMarco. I'm sorry, Mr. Malcolm."

ˋ Because Sergio was new to LADS and the Thursday night LADSrap, I reminded him and the group that we came together to become smart and sexually empowered in our discussions and interactions. I reminded him and the group of our community agreements, specifically number eight, respect is important—sometimes we're the only supporters we have, before returning to the conversation about videos, future goals, and how current decisions they made could impact all of it.

DeMarco, just to make a point to the group's newcomer, recited the LADS community agreements, or steps to becoming a smart, culturally empowered, and sexually empowered young man:

1. LADS will learn to make smart and sexually empowered decisions for their lives and health.
2. LADS have the right to say no. No one is entitled to sex or a hook-up, no matter what they gave to or bought for you.
3. LADS respect that "No Means No" and never force, coerce, pressure someone into sex against their will.
4. LADS have a right to ask and know his sexual health status, the right to insist on condoms at all times, and the responsibility to know and disclose your health status. (That doesn't mean you're dirty if you request or disclose this.)
5. Just because he's a top (and you are), or just because he's a bottom (and you are) doesn't mean you two can't have a meaningful and long-term sexual or romantic relationship.
6. LADS don't have to give him your online passwords, account numbers, or a rundown of your schedule when you're not with him. Possession does not equal love—it might equal crazy.
7. Being smart, culturally empowered, and sexually empowered LADS means knowing who you are, but refusing to be confined by that knowledge.
8. LADS respect each other—sometimes we're the only supporters we have.
9. LADS support the brotherhood and aren't complicit in in tearing down the brotherhood by sleeping with, or getting involved with, men who are involved with someone else.
10. Love yourself. Remember your Black, LGBT, and

Black LGBT history and elders by building upon their legacy of struggle and excellence.

After DeMarco's reiteration of our rules, I continued with the discussion of videos and the future.

"Anyway, my point is that anything you make public about your life—emails or texts you've sent with pics, status updates, or any videos you've posted with your secret sexual talents can come back to haunt you," I said and looked around the room at the participants. "And did you know any job or school you apply for can read your online sites to see if you're someone they want?"

A couple of the guys wrote down notes (or were they texting?) during my talk, as DeMarco chimed in from across the room.

"Guys, I once made the mistake of answering one of those Fredslist ads back in my young and wild days of nineteen… not that I'm *not* young now," he said and laughed. "And next thing I know, *my* picture ends up being used by all sorts of old men trying to attract young, cute men to their houses. It wasn't cute."

"I bet it wasn't," I said. "So I'm sure some of you know someone who has been burned by something they put online… Anyone got a story?"

"Do you have one, Mr. Malcolm?" Sergio said and smiled. "I'd love to hear about Mr. Malcolm's online sexcapades."

Some of the young men chuckled and perked up in their seats while waiting for my response. It was like this every week, no matter the topic, for conversation to lead eventually back to me. I knew it was a sign they cared and were learning something. However, looking back on the meeting three days earlier, my response now came to haunt me.

"Sorry, gentlemen," I'd said and smiled. "But I would never do anything online that would harm or hurt my career or reputation. I've worked too hard for that. And I would hope you'd do the same with all the hard work you're doing for your future goals."

What a hypocrite three days can make.

As I pulled in front of *his* apartment complex, I said a little prayer. I'm not a super-religious person, but I knew calling in the wisdom and positive energy of a higher power was the only thing that would save *him* and keep me from being the top story on the eleven o'clock news.

CHAPTER 3

It wasn't that Deacon and I had a particularly bad breakup. Deacon is "him," by the way.

He and I could have remained friends, maybe even remained together, if not for the one he left me for. I don't even like mentioning his name—the one Deacon left me for, or Deacon, for that matter. So I generally don't mention his name unless there's no other choice. Still, I couldn't imagine why he would put our sex life on the Internet.

Deacon and I had two strong years together before things ended. We met when he was hired as a security guard at the bank where I worked before jumping into the world of social services and LADS. One of those community organizations that give young men in trouble second chances referred him to the bank's minority outreach program, which I chaired.

Seeing that I was on the hiring committee, and chaired the minority outreach program that selected Deacon, I never should have crossed that line—and Kyle advised me from a legal perspective it was bad news—personally or professionally. But that security guard uniform, combined with the mystery of his blue collar life, brought out the Mother Teresa in me. I had to know more, thought we were doing the right thing by giving him a job and a chance in life, and soon found myself looking forward to the days he was scheduled to work in the bank.

Deacon told captivating stories and kept the professional staff all smiles during the day, which definitely kept our minds off the fact that he'd come to the bank through one of those organizations that gave troubled twenty-somethings a second chance in life. So I ignored family and friend advice about people never *really* leaving trouble behind, and took a chance during a work-related Friday happy hour. I put it out there in one of those truth-or-dare games young professionals play at happy hour that if I *had* to do another guy on staff at the bank, it would be Deacon the security guard. Two martinis will loosen you up and make you say anything. A late night sext/text message from Deacon the security guard will loosen you up, make you throw professionalism to the wind and your legs up in the air.

A year into our relationship, which we kept quiet to the people at the bank, my father died. That threw my world into disarray for a few months. I went back to Indiana to help with all the family decisions, and while there, decided to make some career changes in my life. None of these changes, I thought, necessarily affected Deacon, but nonetheless, he blamed them for our demise as a couple.

I decided to start LADS after reading what seemed like the millionth news story dooming the men of my community to a life of unemployment, incarceration, disease, illiteracy, or any other social malady. I jumped right in and decided to do something. No social work degree, just a business undergrad degree from Northwestern University and a liberal, kind heart and mind. No experience running a social services agency. But I knew something needed to be done, and done quickly, to address the issues facing my community. And since I had the means to do so, I acted on my compulsion. Maybe a little bit too quickly.

I quit my job at the bank going after delinquent customers and accounts and decided to use my life in a different way. Figured it was time to live up to my namesakes, Malcolm and Martin. Took the vacation, retirement, and severance money the bank job offered, combined it with the insurance my father left me and the grant money I'd applied for from the city and state, and started my own community organization. I named it LADS, in honor of the name my dad affectionately called me up until the time he died. I found a decent-sized space on Crenshaw Boulevard, south of the 10 freeway, in the heart of Black L.A., where I felt a group like this was needed. I just wanted to do something good and give back.

The plan was for LADS to offer personal, group, and career counseling, GED training, AIDS/HIV/health education, food vouchers, and a non-judgmental space for dealing with sex and sexuality issues. It was an organization for young men coming of age, and coming out of the closet. Yeah, *that* closet. Young, gay Black men.

Everyone thought I was crazy when I opened LADS, including my best friend Kyle and my family. Kyle couldn't understand giving up a stable nine-to-five for a job with unpredictable hours that required some nights and weekends. My mother thought the young men I wanted to save weren't savable and I was wasting the money our father left behind. My sister Marlena liked the idea, but worried for both my and the young men's safety, since being young, gay, and from the inner city was a concept "we just don't talk about," including her son Blake.

Deacon worried our relationship away, thinking that every time I had a planning meeting for LADS, it was really a secret rendezvous with someone else. Once, he said he liked us working together so he could keep an eye on me and my schedule. So paranoid and threatened by my dream. But it turned out his paranoia was an indication of his own guilt about his own secret flings outside our relationship. That is another story for another time, but the words he spewed to me when I found out about his cheating stung forever: "Sorry, Malcolm, it just be's that way sometime with us guys from the 'hood."

I regularly tell the young men in LADS this: If you're doing something positive—and really working at it, not just daydreaming of it—and he's not supportive because he's thinking only of *his* needs, while it can hurt to call it quits, you're better off. Better to be single and alone than alone in a relationship. I hope they listen to me, because it's the truth.

Something I knew I wouldn't get from Deacon.

"Deacon," I yelled outside his apartment door. Well, his new young boyfriend's apartment, where Deacon moved after we split up. "Open the damn door, you loser."

It was just off the swimming pool courtyard of the complex near Vermont and the 101 freeway, in a very working-class neighborhood. Like where people rode bikes and buses more than their own cars. I'd helped him move his few garbage bags of belongings here after the "it just be's that way" conversation so he could *be* with his boy toy.

I wasn't usually a fan of causing a scene, but knowing my sex life was now fodder for any voyeur around the world with a computer warranted one. A young couple and their toddler looked up from their pool-wading session to watch the commotion I was causing. I knocked, well, BANGED on the door continuously for two minutes until Deacon answered. I knew he had to be there. His bike was chained to his front porch railing, and that 1999 Maxima he just had to have, and I bought for him, was still sitting on cinder blocks out front—a reminder that Deacon the social-program loser never did follow up on anything, including fixing and repainting the car to sell at a profit.

When he opened his apartment door, I could see he was still living in luxurious bachelor-pad splendor. Pitiful, being twenty eight years old and being sprung by a twenty-two-year-old with no decorating taste. And if twenty-two did have taste, he most certainly didn't have the ability or means to act on it. Bricks and cinder blocks served as a bookcase with no books, and a coffee table used more as a footrest than for coffee or knickknacks were the largest pieces of "furniture" in the room. Incense burned, irritating my eyes. An old tan futon, one that was in the spare bedroom of my apartment when I let him live with me, sat against the living room wall and was pulled out as a bed. I could hear Sade playing in the background. Clearly he was setting the mood for a romantic night with his new man, or maybe yet another man, who knew?

"What the fuck is your problem, Malcolm?" Deacon asked angrily. His do-rag strings flung side to side as he yelled. He was dressed in plain white boxers only and was happily dangling left down there. Yes, I looked. He looked good as always. Dark brown, lean, and lovely, in that way that non-gym-going guys from the 'hood look who don't have to work out or watch what they eat. "And why are you here?"

"I'm here to fuck you up," I said and did something I wasn't raised to do. I socked him across the jaw. So much for the hand of God calming me or my tongue. Lord knows where that came from.

"Aww, snap," he said. He rubbed where I'd hit him and stood stunned. I expected a return hit to come any second. So far, nothing. "Where you learn that move?"

"Chris Brown," I said.

"Damn, boy," he said. "You getting a little street cred from the boys, huh?"

"And you're gonna get a lot more if you don't take those videos down from GayClick," I said.

"Get in here." He grabbed me inside the apartment and yelled outside to the happy family by the pool, "It's cool, y'all. It's cool. He don't know what he talking about." Slammed the door behind us.

"They already know you're gay," I said. "Stop the DL act. That's so 2005."

"You're sexy when you're mad, Malcolm," Deacon said and smiled, attempting to be charming. He moved in closer to me, rubbed his face against mine, and whispered in my ear. "You make me wanna bend you over a chair and take you from behind like I used to."

I pushed him away from me. Maybe I had developed some street credibility since working with the young men at LADS. I'd certainly heard and seen it all since starting the work.

"I'm not playing...and I'm not here to sleep with you. Where are they?" I asked as I looked around the living room. Opened up the nearest hallway closet. "Where are the cameras?"

"Huh? What cameras?"

"The ones you used to videotape our sex life, you dumb fuck," I yelled. "The ones you kept hidden in my apartment to record us...doing things."

"Dang, Malcolm. Active imagination," he said. "What story you been watching?"

"This isn't a game. It's my *life*."

"I don't know what you're talking about."

"Videos of what we used to do when we were together," I said. "Some in your old apartment. Most from my bedroom. If I had known you were taping us, I *never* would have consented. Didn't our time together mean anything to you?"

"Of course you meant a lot, Malcolm, but how do you

know about any cameras or videotapes?" Deacon said. "That was my own private collection…for memories."

"It was our sex life, and it was meant to be private."

"And it is private, Malcolm," Deacon said and opened his laptop. "I keep them all in a password-protected file, just for me to get off on once in a while."

Once the screen lit and Deacon accessed his videos, I saw my secret and dirty past come to life. He'd saved almost two hundred videos, videos I never knew he was making. Filed, very simply, with each of his previous boyfriends before me, with easy-to-understand headings: ass, jack, oral.

I was disgusted.

When we were together and I loved Deacon, I had no problem sharing or showing him how much I loved him. We did it safely and we did it often. That's what couples are supposed to do when they're in love and like each other. But they don't videotape without permission.

"Who else has access to your computer?" I asked. "What about the kid you live with? Has he seen these? You videotape him?"

"I never showed him. He has his own laptop. Yes, I make movies of us."

"Well, someone has or had access to your computer, or else I wouldn't be all over the Internet looking like a…never mind," I said. "I need you to think really hard…a computer repair person, your little boyfriend, one of your or his friends?"

I asked Deacon to get up so I could see the evidence of our past together. He did, and I pointed and clicked at random video files. Just to see the Deacon and Malcolm show. In a way, I was ashamed of the video archive. I'd always been the good boy, the good son, the one who made everything right and did the right thing. I was trying to teach gay young men how to live their lives with dignity and esteem, including their relationships and sex lives. Seeing myself acting like a porn star, albeit with my at-the-time boyfriend, was something I couldn't quite reconcile. I felt like a living paradox.

"Deacon, I have never been more disappointed than I am right now," I said. "Why would you do something like this without my consent? Do you want to go back to almost-on-probation life?"

"I'm sorry," he said. "I'll delete everything with you in it. Is that cool?"

"The damage has been done," I said. "Oh, and by the way, whoever uploaded those videos only put the ones where I'm visible and you're not. Pretty slick and deliberate move, I'd say."

"I'm sorry, babe," Deacon said and tried to reach for me. So sexy, but I wasn't falling. Not this time. "Can I make it up? Break you off some before he comes home?"

"You're duplicitous," I said. "I have lost the last bit of respect I had for you, Deacon."

"What?"

"Look it up," I said.

"Snap."

"I guess *we* didn't mean anything to you?"

He stood silent.

And then I said the words I vowed never to say to anyone and that most Black men I know never want to hear, especially from someone they were or are close to.

"You ain't *shit*, Deacon. You'll never amount to anything."

He put his hands around his face and nodded in disagreement. Like he was trying to figure out something. Like there was any way to fix my soon-to-be damaged reputation. Like he really cared anymore. I had to remind myself that Deacon left me because he was threatened by my latest career move with LADS.

"I'll be right back. Gonna run to the bathroom."

"Fine, I'm out," I said. "You didn't keep any backup files or videos anywhere else?"

"Nah, once I finally got them all on my computer, I destroyed everything. They take up too much space. There's nothing else."

"Fine."

Deacon disappeared from the living room. I waited until I heard the bathroom door close behind him before I got started. Knew I had to work quickly, before Deacon returned and before his new boyfriend caught me.

I removed the cord attaching the laptop to the wall plug. I picked up the laptop and carried it to the front door. The young family that was wading in the pool when I arrived was nowhere to be found, which relieved me. Deacon and I probably scared them off. Good, no risk to them.

And with an ease that surprised me, I, the good boy, the good son, the one who made everything right and did the right thing, did something not so right.

I tossed Deacon's laptop into the swimming pool, watched it sink to the bottom, and gave a friendly hello to Deacon's new, young, and cute boyfriend as we passed each other through the apartment complex gates.

CHAPTER 4

Yes, I really did throw his computer in the pool," I said. "Oh my God, Malcolm," Kyle said. "You're crazy. I really mean it."

It was Monday morning, and I was in L.A.'s stop-and-go traffic going about twenty miles an hour. Days like this I thanked God my Prius was good on gas. My Bluetooth was perched on top of my left ear, both hands on the steering wheel, except for occasional bites of my morning McMuffin. I hadn't had time to fix anything for breakfast. The drivers to the left and right of me were also having Bluetooth conversations. Always something to be done or talked about in L.A. For me, it was catching up with Kyle before I got to LADS and before he got to the television and film lot in Culver City where he worked as an executive.

"I will admit it's a little out of character for me," I said.

"A little?" Kyle laughed. "Good boys from Indiana don't do things like that. Psych!"

"And yes, I feel a little bad," I said. "I know he probably can't afford another laptop right away."

"Fuck that, Malcolm, he owns cameras small enough to videotape you when you don't know it," Kyle said. "He'll figure it out. These young bucks always find ways to afford stuff they shouldn't."

"True," I said. Kyle did have a point. "Fuck that."

"Aren't you worried he'll call the police or something?"

"And say what?" I said. "Hmm, 'Officer, my ex tossed my computer in the pool because I was secretly videotaping our sex life for two years without his knowledge.' Yeah, right."

"Point taken, girl. You're a mess."

"I'm not a girl, but a woman," I said and laughed, trying to make a heavy moment light. "But what still pisses me off is how nonchalant Deacon was about the whole thing. Like it's a normal, everyday thing to make sex tapes without your partner's consent."

"He was really that chill about it?" Kyle asked. "Wait, all the kids are whatever about technology."

"I mean, he said 'sorry' a few times," I said. "But he didn't offer to help get the videos removed from the website. He didn't even have any idea how anyone got the files off his computer, though I think his little punk boyfriend did it. Or maybe Deacon did it. Who knows?"

I grabbed my McMuffin when traffic came to a complete stop again.

"No doubt. People will do anything these days. No shame."

"He didn't even apologize for videotaping me without my permission," I said. "The whole thing makes me sick. I'm just hoping the website honored my request and took the videos down. I emailed and called the site administrator last night and this morning. I don't want to have to explain this to the people at work. If the kids at LADS, not to mention the advisory board…"

"No doubt," Kyle said. "But just so you know, I have no desire to check the website. You and your sex life…T-M-I, you know?"

"Gee, Kyle, thank you for not being a perv."

We laughed. Brought some minor relief to my situation. I knew as soon as I got to work, I'd check my email and see a message from the website administrator confirming that my sex tapes would be off the Internet. Though I had no idea how long the videos had been online, in my mind I prayed-hoped-wished that guy from The Abbey, Compton and his group of friends, were the only ones to see them. Unlikely. But wishful thinking nonetheless.

"Well, I'm about to pull into the studio lot," Kyle said. "Another day of trying to find America's next big television hit."

"Cool, thanks for listening to me vent," I said. "I appreciate it, best friend."

"Of course," he said. "I'll hit you up later this morning."

"Maybe I can meet up with you and Bernard after work?" I said. "I have a few days before my 'single' days are over. My nephew's coming this weekend."

"That's right, Blake, the gay rapper," he said.

"Yes, Blake," I said. "That's a whole 'nother story. But we'll talk."

"We'll talk," Kyle said. "I'm at security check-in. Bye."

I continued my trek west on the 10 freeway. So close to the Crenshaw exit, yet so far, traveling five miles an hour now. The perfect speed for people watching my car neighbors on the freeway.

Wondered if any of them had seen my sex tapes on GayClick. Somewhat relieved that soon the videos would be removed from the Internet, if they hadn't been removed already.

CHAPTER 5

There are days when I think my friends and family might be right and that I've gotten in over my head with LADS.

Being on call has its trade-offs, and you never know what you'll deal with next—a young man gets put out of the family home or gets beat up outside a club or on the gay ho-stroll in the middle of the night, and you're required to be there if you get the call.

Sometimes you wonder if the stat—is it one in four, three, or two?—is in fact true and that it's not a question of "if" but "when" the young men you're working with will be diagnosed HIV-positive.

Sometimes you wonder if they'll end up in jail or prison for some nonviolent crime of survival.

Sometimes you wonder if you, alone, can do what the community-at-large and politicians have not done.

Sometimes you wonder when LADS will be self-sustaining and you'll no longer have to dip into reserves or sink your own money into it. Even though it's a nonprofit, the budget still needs to balance by the end of the fiscal year. The board of directors the city requires you to have makes sure you have a balanced budget and that you're operating within city and state regulations for a community organization.

You know that every day brings you another piece of

anonymous hate mail or an "article" full of religious quotes and human interpretations of your impending doom, debates from local clergy, telephoned threats of violence, a stinging newspaper editorial that you're airing the dirty laundry of your community, or disapproving looks from the underemployed men who sit at the pay phone outside your office all day or the church secretary who strolls by at noon for her lunchtime walk.

I pulled into the parking lot of LADS and willed myself to put all those negative and worrisome thoughts out my head. Put on my game face. Big smile. Optimism. Keeping a refreshed look. Being the leader my community and constituents at LADS wanted and needed me to be. I called it putting on my "Hillary," whom I admired greatly, and who I figured went through a lot privately but still got up and fought for that 2008 campaign and those causes that mattered to her.

After all, my name is Malcolm. Malcolm Martin Campbell. Talk about high expectations, being named after two of the most prolific and well-quoted leaders of Black community politics—Malcolm X and Martin Luther King Jr. Makes me wonder what my mother envisioned for my sister Marlena, with her being named after my mom's favorite soap opera character from *Days of Our Lives*, Dr. Marlena Evans. Did she want a doctor? Or did she want a long-suffering heroine?

When I entered the lobby area of LADS, I was *not* greeted by my front desk assistant, DeMarco, who was wearing the oversized sunglasses I'd told him not to wear inside while working. He called them a necessity. For what, I didn't know, because he was far from being the Jackie Onassis fashionista he thought he was, and he definitely was not visually impaired. I'd told DeMarco that if he *needed* this job, like I knew he did, then the shades were a negative.

DeMarco came to LADS after a violent relationship

with a possessive man old enough to be his father, who left him on life support and without any of the material goods he'd collected during his time with the man. Penniless, with no clothes, no shelter, and no real marketable skills. I found DeMarco to be very energetic with a fatherly wit beyond his twenty years. An old soul, as they call the type. Found a family to take him in for a few months, put him in training for office managerial work, and offered him an entry-level job at the front desk of LADS.

He was behind the desk with the *L.A. Times* sports section open and his eyes on the computer monitor. Hard to believe he could read the screen with those sunglasses on. I also heard that Rihanna music that was a part of DeMarco's personal social media page, which I'd told him was another no-no while at work.

As I got closer, I could see he'd been reading a newspaper profile on Tyrell Kincaid, the professional basketball player who'd recently been outed by some radical gay and lesbian activist group due to his ongoing friendship/relationship with R&B singer Tommie Jordan, though Jordan's camp denied the reports and Kincaid's camp was silent on the matter. I didn't believe any of the speculation, especially when it came from hard-core activists whose main agenda seemed to be making people angry rather than making people whole or solving problems. I heard the guys in LADS gossiping daily about which rapper or actor they wanted to be gay, or about someone they knew who had supposedly dated a celebrity. All the gays had fantasies of turning out a famous person. I thought it was all ridiculous—wanting someone out of your league and who you could never have—and I was glad I hadn't bought into too much of L.A.'s obsession with celebrity.

One of the things I'd tried to get the staff and clients of LADS to do was spend less time online and more time reading newspapers, books, and magazines for their information. Not that they couldn't do the same with the Internet. To me, it just somehow felt more real to pick up a piece of paper and read versus pointing, clicking, and browsing. Well, I guess we did the same with a newspaper, but still. I chalked it up to the generational differences between those in their twenties and those who were older.

I cleared my throat. "Good morning, DeMarco," I said.

"Oh, um, good morning, Malcolm," he said. "How was your weekend?"

"It was…"

"Mine was off the hook," he said with a large smile on his face. He loved showing off his new braces, courtesy of the dental plan he was now able to take advantage of through his job. "I met the finest dude online, and he made me spaghetti, and we kicked it at his place, and he drove me around in his new ride…a BMW 5-series. I think I'm in love."

"You're always in love, DeMarco," I said and chuckled. "My weekend was okay, thanks for asking. Got a little situation I'm trying to solve, but otherwise…"

"Did you know Tyrell Kincaid bought a house for that woman with eight kids whose house burned down this spring? Not the Octomom, but a sista with two sets of twins and four other kids…all under ten years old." DeMarco folded up the newspaper article like he'd *just* finished it right when I walked in the door. The A-D-D-ness of it all, how DeMarco could change subjects like nothing, but it still made sense…to him.

"Nice try, DeMarco. I know," I said. "I also know you're online for something other than work. I hear your music."

"Busted," he said. Smiled. Good kid, but twenty, and still thought he was smarter than those older than he. "But I am working too. I'm reading about Tyrell Kincaid, and you haven't seen the community room yet, have you?"

"Not yet. Are we set up for Tyrell's keynote talk tonight?"
"All done, Malcolm," he said and smiled. And then took
down his shades. "My bad."

"Mmmmm-hmmmm."

"Desiree's bringing the catering from Watts Coffee House
by five fifteen, Tyrell should be here at five fifty, doors open at
six, Tyrell starts at six fifteen."

He pulled out his planner with a partially completed
checklist for the evening's keynote address. I was impressed.
Maybe he had been learning from his work at LADS.

"Wow, you're on top of it," I said. "You must really be in
love. Getting your work done early and actually finishing it.
What time did you come in?"

"I was here by seven," he said. "I have a reason to wake
up in the morning, now that I've got this job...and my new
man."

I wanted to reply with, "Whom you've known for just
two days," but didn't want to deflate his young feelings about
his new lover. Been there, done that enough to know that next
Monday when I came to work, DeMarco would be talking
about a new lover. Ahh, the curse and benefit of being a new
kid on the scene...as soon as you lost flavor for one, you'd
surely pick up another. Just. Like. That.

Instead, I replied, "Good for you, DeMarco. I hope this
one works out."

"I'm sure it will," he said. "In fact, I told him about the
Tyrell Kincaid event here and he said he'd stop by."

"It's RSVP only, remember."

"I got connections, Malcolm, I'm the RSVP system," he
said and smiled. Held up his clipboard with the names of guests
and donors who'd called in to attend. Those names, I had my
police officer friend Omar Etheridge run a quick background
check on, just in case any crazies decided to attend.

"Fine," I said. "I'ma be in my office if you need anything. No messages?"

"Just the usual, boss," he said. "I got this all taken care of. But I want you to look at the community room and how I set it up. I hope you like it."

"I will," I said. "And I'm sure I'll like it. You do good work around here, DeMarco."

"Awww, thanks. I love my job."

I grabbed mail from my inbox behind the reception desk and walked down the hall to check on the community room. Along the way, I checked to make sure DeMarco had vacuumed extra thoroughly and that he had straightened out the pictures and posters along the wall. Check.

DeMarco had done beyond a good job getting the community room ready for Tyrell Kincaid's talk. He'd done an excellent job, and I would be sure to note that in my introduction for the event and in DeMarco's next job evaluation. Catering tables in place, with Sternos ready for Watts Coffee House's soul food delivery. Chairs lined up in neat rows. Black and gold chair covers and bows in place. Crisply creased programs, featuring an agenda and biographical information on Tyrell Kincaid, on the chairs. Podium with the LADS logo in place and the sound equipment ready to go. All we needed were the flower arrangements featuring Tyrell's team's colors on both sides of the podium later in the day and we'd be set.

I was amazed and happy that there was one less thing for me to worry about thanks to the work DeMarco had done that morning. Days like this, when a major event was scheduled to happen at LADS, could turn my normally calm and centered personality into an unpredictable and crazy one. And the guys didn't like that side of me.

Before sitting down to write my introduction of Tyrell Kincaid on my work computer, I pulled out my personal laptop to take a look at the GayClick website. I wanted to make sure the videos featuring me were no longer active on the site. Not the kind of thing I wanted lingering for more people to see.

And as I'd requested, there were no more videos of me on the site. I checked and cross-checked under any possible category they could have been filed under. Nothing. Relieved, I packed away my personal laptop, hung up the garment bag that contained the suit and tie I'd change into for the Tyrell Kincaid event in the evening.

Sent up a silent prayer of thanks that I would no longer have to worry about seeing myself on pornographic websites. Little miracles happened every day, and this was proof that the day would indeed be a good one.

CHAPTER 6

The event with Tyrell Kincaid went off perfectly from start to finish. From Tyrell's arrival and handling, to the seating for LADS guests and donors, to how the guys who received services from LADS acted during the event, I couldn't complain.

What I specifically appreciated was that Tyrell talked about all the things that I'd asked him to address—areas important to the mission of LADS: personal responsibility, empowerment, integrity, and care for self and community. They were all messages I emphasized in my work. While the young men appeared to listen to me, they *really* listened to Tyrell Kincaid, tall, dark, hip, handsome, smart, pro basketball player. They, in their Black and Queer glory and diversity: hip-hop hardness, baseball hats, jerseys, bald fades, side-part comb-overs, 42-inch sew-in weaves, skinny jeans, ultra-plucked eyebrows that looked like McDonald's arches, quarter-sized hickeys on the neck like fast-food "may I take your order" front-line restaurant workers, and lip gloss.

In fact, Tyrell was a hit with the boys—well, *young men.* In addition to sharing his message of hope and inspiration, he gave them all new iPods as well as gift cards to pick up a free pair of Kincaid sneakers at a local athletic shoe store. Everyone was surprised and happy with the gifts.

As many in the crowd lingered around the buffet table of various soul food dishes for a reception, I pulled Tyrell aside near the podium. In addition to wanting to give him his honorarium for speaking, I wanted to share my personal thanks for his time at LADS.

"No need for thanks, Malcolm," he said in response to my greeting. "I'm happy to do this. We need more places like this in our neighborhoods, and we need men like you giving these young guys some guidance. I think if I'd had a place like this when I was growing up, I'd have made different choices with life, relationships, all of it."

"I was surprised when you agreed to come," I said. "I mean, pro basketball players aren't exactly known for their social justice and political stances, especially around issues of sexual orientation. And I wasn't sure if you'd be comfortable talking about your personal experience."

"Then you must not know much about me," Tyrell said. "Outside of the gossip and hearsay...and the stereotypes you hear about pro-ballers."

I wished I hadn't opened my big mouth with an awkward and sweeping statement about athletes. I'm sure he'd heard that and more during his athletic career. I didn't know much about basketball players. I could have admitted that I barely knew who Tyrell was until I'd Googled him after some of the young men at LADS mentioned him during one of our LADSrap meetings a few months earlier.

Learned that Tyrell Kincaid grew up in Washington, D.C., in a middle-class household with both parents, double majored in English and African American Studies at UCLA, earned his degree while playing basketball for the university, and had had a mediocre career in the NBA, having sat on the bench for four of the five teams he'd been traded to in the past five years. Also learned that he was twenty-six and perpetually single, though some of the gossipier websites and those bitter gay activist types tried to link him to this one R&B singer, Tommie Jordan. I'd heard the rumors among friends, especially from Kyle, who swore it based on his connections in the entertainment industry, but never knew what to believe and not to believe. So I left it alone.

"My apologies," I said. Tried to smile off the awkwardness as much as I could. "Anyway, it was nice having someone of your status to talk to my guys."

"No apology needed, man," he said and stuck out his hand to fist-bump mine. "I deal with nervous people all the time who say foot-in-mouth things to me. I have that effect on people, I hear."

I smiled. It was nice Tyrell was so down-to-earth and well-spoken. Modest. If not for his fame, I could have seen us being friends in another time and place, like if I were nine years younger and went to UCLA instead of Northwestern where maybe we would have crossed paths.

"Anyway, Tyrell, here's your honorarium," I said and reached into my portfolio sitting next to the podium. "It's not much, but it's our token of appreciation for your time."

"Cool," he said and looked at the check I was embarrassed to write him. "Wow, the low three digits. Plus a signing bonus of thirty cents. That'll buy a nice dinner out, huh?"

"Okay, don't clown me at my work. I hardly know you."

"Then get to know me," he said. "Let me use this honorarium to meet you for dinner sometime."

"What? Huh? Me?"

"Nah, man, I mean your young assistant with the stunna shades over there," he said pointing to DeMarco. "You...if it's cool. I'm a little famous, but I'm normal. I eat. I talk."

I was a little surprised that Tyrell wanted to hang out with me, but figured it would be a good opportunity to network for the benefit of LADS. Securing a new donor, and one of Tyrell's status and fame, would be a coup and secure me additional brownie points with the board of directors. We needed to shore up our reserves for long-term planning for the organization.

"Sure," I said. "Name the time and place and I'm there."

"I'll give you a ring here at the center," he said and handed me one of his business cards. "Or you call me. And we're in business."

And with that, our business for the day was done, and I had a pending dinner meeting with Tyrell Kincaid.

CHAPTER 7

S o were you pleased with the day, DeMarco?"
I knew he was, and I was too, but just wanted to hear
DeMarco share it in his own words so that he could see how
he'd contributed to a successful event with Tyrell Kincaid. We
were winding down the day at LADS. We'd just cleaned up the
community room and were shutting off lights in the computer
lab. I liked debriefing events after they finished so that our
feedback and memories were fresh of what worked and didn't.

"Of course," he said. He showed off his new braces with
a huge smile. "I never met anyone famous before, and Tyrell
was real cool…real down-to-earth, ya dig."

"Yeah, he was an approachable guy," I said. "I never met
anyone famous either. I was a little nervous too."

"I saw him trying to throw game at you, Malcolm," he said
and laughed. "You better do it like them gold-digger women
and get yourself pregnant by a baller."

"Funny," I said. "But we all know one thing…"

"Butt babies don't live, okaaaay," DeMarco said and
laughed. "That's nature's birth control for the gays. Can't
imagine how many times I woulda been pregnant by now, if
the gays could get pregnant."

DeMarco often used the gay pregnancy analogy during his

LADSrap sessions, which, surprisingly, worked when getting the young men to think about and insist on safe sex.

"But anyway, that talk with Tyrell was all networking," I said. "We might meet for a business lunch or something to see if Tyrell might want a long-standing relationship with LADS."

"Hmmph," DeMarco said. "Long-standing relationship with the *founder* of LADS is more like it. I wasn't born yesterday, just the late eighties." He put his fist out to bump mine, which I did.

"I've had more yesterdays than you," I said and smiled. "And I can tell you that everyone who talks one-on-one with you isn't doing it for the possibility of romance."

"Malcolm, you are on his radar."

"Oh please," I said. "It's all business. And I'm ready to shut it down for the day."

We closed up the computer lab, set the alarm codes, and walked to the back door that exited to the parking lot. I noticed a shiny silver BMW parked next to my Prius.

"That's my man," DeMarco said. "Right on time to get his boo. I got him trained right."

"Lucky you," I said. "Next time he'll have to stop by to see the good work you do."

"I'm about to show him the good work I do in another way," he said and sashayed to his new boyfriend's car. He blew me a kiss. "See you tomorrow, boss."

He was off, just like that. No polite introduction, like people would normally do…just because it was the polite thing to do. Then again, romance among the young was a temporary, fleeting thing. Always someone new to be introduced to…so why go through the motions every other week?

As DeMarco and his man peeled off out of the parking lot, I realized that an introduction might not have been necessary after all. I caught a glimpse of the driver as they drove past me, and saw the name on the personalized license place. Coincidence or not?

It was Compton.

At least I thought it was Compton, but I decided not to trip on it. At least not at the moment. I could always ask DeMarco about his new boyfriend the next day.

After all, it had been a great day at LADS. And it was time to hang out with Kyle and Bernard for some after-work drinks and dinner.

CHAPTER 8

I knew the spread that sat before us had nothing to do with Kyle or his culinary skills.

Having been his best friend since college, I knew Kyle had a close and intimate relationship with any and all takeout menus he could get his hands on. Eight years earlier when he met and partnered off with Bernard, who jokingly called himself a Black, gay Martha Stewart-Washington-Jackson-Jones, Kyle and I both knew he'd hit the jackpot. Kyle didn't have a domestic bone in his body.

"Bernard got called to fill in for the raw cooking class," Kyle said. "Instructor got sick…food poisoning."

"And that's why you'll never catch me eating raw, except maybe for sushi," I said as I sat at the picnic table on the screened-in back porch. What Kyle lacked in culinary skills, he compensated for in setting ambience. Flameless candles flickered on the table, and the glow of white lanterns shone down from above. By the time the sun completely set, it would look like we were sitting in a sea of stars.

In front of us sat the most colorful and delicious-looking summer meal. Definitely California cuisine. An avocado, tomato, onion concoction in individual lettuce leaves, a cold black-eyed-peas salad, Bernard's famous fruit soup in scooped-out cantaloupe shells, and a pitcher of white-wine sangria. Why the Food Network had never green-lit a show for Bernard, after three auditions, was beyond me. Bernard was the best cook—raw, fried, grilled, or otherwise—I'd known. And he was funny too, and so good to my best friend. I sent up a silent prayer request for a partner skilled in cooking, and also sent up a silent thank-you for the meal I was about to receive. I hadn't eaten any of the food at the Tyrell Kincaid event—running around, organizing, making sure everyone was happy—so I was hungry.

"Don't knock it 'til you try it," Kyle said. "That's how Bernard and I lost all that weight last summer. It works."

"No thanks," I said. The thought of going one hundred percent raw wasn't appealing at all, though I did admire Kyle and Bernard's weight loss they'd managed to maintain in the past year. "So no Bernard tonight...I'm bummed."

"I'm that terrible to hang out with, I know...thanks, Malcolm," he said, and held up his glass of sangria. "Cheers to good food and fellowship."

"Cheers," I said, clinked glasses, and drank. "Mmm, this is good and strong. The way I like my drinks."

Kyle and I loved a good drink, dating back to our young and innocent days at Northwestern University. At that time, our cocktail repertoire consisted of anything mixed with Kool-Aid. Dorm life, combined with no money and no cultural capital, you improvise. Luckily, since then, we'd graduated and upgraded to much better cocktails. After graduation, Kyle had been offered an overnight producer job in the newsroom at the CBS affiliate in L.A. I hadn't found a job worthy of my business degree yet, and the idea of living without my best friend was something I didn't want to do at age twenty-two, so I moved to California with Kyle. We shared a two-bedroom near the TV station for a couple of years, while I got established at the bank and while Kyle worked at the station and finished law school. We both got used to life in L.A. Though living in separate places, and with totally different lives, new jobs, and multiple boyfriends along the way, Kyle and I did our best to hang out a few times a week.

"So tell me about your day…you had Tyrell Kincaid as a speaker, right?"

What Kyle lacked in culinary skills, he made up for in listening skills too. Most of the time.

I shared Tyrell's major themes in his speech, details about the catering from Watts Coffee House, how happy I was with DeMarco's coordination work, and finally how I thought DeMarco's new boyfriend was Compton, the man who brought those videos to my attention at The Abbey the previous night.

"But I'm not so worried if he is or isn't DeMarco's new man," I said. "The videos are gone off GayClick. It'd be my word against Compton's…not that I'm wanting an ultimatum or confrontation kind of situation with my worker. So let's change the subject."

"Like to Tyrell Kincaid…yum," Kyle said and sucked on his bottom lip. "I've only seen him once in person, and that was at a distance on the red carpet at a movie premiere."

"He's a looker," I said and smiled. If I'd had lighter skin, I'm sure I would have been red from thinking about Tyrell. "And I've never met anyone that tall…and those fingers."

"You and your finger fetish…freak," Kyle said. "No wonder you're making ho videos all over the Internet."

We laughed. Then stopped suddenly and stared at each other. It was a way we had with things that were funny, but not really funny, but kinda funny. Another one of our you-had-to-know-us-at-Northwestern moments.

"At least those Internet moments were with my boyfriend, and I wasn't being paid to do it with strangers."

"Oh, I'm not knocking it," Kyle said. "Nothing wrong

with being an intellectual slut. An academic top. A bookworm bottom. It's all good to me, girl."

"I like to call it 'smart and sexually empowered,'" I said. "At least that's how I try to teach it to the guys at LADS."

"Semantics," Kyle said. "I'm the lawyer."

"Anyway, Tyrell is a very nice and smart guy, in addition to being good-looking," I said. "And the guys at LADS loved him."

"Too bad his boyfriend doesn't love him."

"What?"

"Don't act like you never heard the rumors about Tyrell Kincaid and that singer Tommie Jordan," Kyle said and finished his glass of sangria. "Best friends, puh-lease."

"You know I'm not into all that gossip."

"I work at Fox...I know people, girl," Kyle said. "Tyrell and Tommie been together for almost five or six unhappy and closeted years."

That was news to me. I always thought those rumors I heard on gossip shows were just that...rumors. I knew Kyle was well-connected and knew loads more celebrity gossip than he shared with me.

"But why unhappy?" I asked. "They're rich and beautiful Black men."

"Well, if Tommie could keep his dick in his pants, Tyrell would be happy," Kyle said and sipped on his sangria. "But you didn't hear that from me."

"I never would have known from how upbeat Tyrell was earlier this evening."

"You *paid* him to be upbeat and motivating to the guys at LADS," Kyle said matter-of-factly. "But anyway, when we finish dinner, we're going to see the source of Tyrell's unhappiness."

"Go somewhere after eating all this food?" I said. I'd

barely started, and Kyle was already pushing an evening of festivities. It was almost nine, and I had work the next morning. "I just wanted to chill here until traffic died down before driving back to Silver Lake...*and* to spend time with my buddies, of course."

"Nice save, bitch," he said. "There's a music showcase this evening at this little underground club in Hollywood. Chrisette Michele, Dwele, Alice Smith, Elle Varner, and Tommie Jordan. Invitation only, industry folks. So it'll be cool."

Of course, the first thing that came to mind was not how fun it would be. After all, I loved Kyle's invitation-only, industry folks events when they fell on Fridays or Saturdays. I thought about work the next morning, if I'd be able to wake up on time if I went to a show, and my never-ending to-do list. And then...

"I'm still dressed for work, Kyle," I said. "I can't be with all your Hollywood friends dressed like a Carlton."

My khaki pants and white button-down shirt were cute to me for work, but would get me mistaken for the help at a Hollywood listening party.

"You're still part of the PBC, right," Kyle said. "I got plenty of clothes for your fat ass."

I giggled at the nickname we'd given ourselves in college when we discovered how much our various crushes, dates, and boyfriends loved the bedroom skills of the Power Bottom Crew. We were quite nasty nerds at Northwestern University. The "fat ass" part, though, was a sore spot for me. I knew I was nowhere near fat at a 170 pounds, but being in L.A. makes you wonder about yourself because you know most people size you up as overweight at size medium. Kyle was back to the same size he was in college, except for a few new muscles put on by his personal trainer. I was happily jealous, but didn't let on, about his new body.

"Sick," I said. "No you didn't go there with the PBC."

"Wait, what am I asking…I saw some of those videos. You're the diamond princess of the PBC."

"Oh my God, are you serious, Kyle?" I asked. "This morning you said you didn't watch, liar."

"You didn't think Bernard and I would just let it pass by without a peek?" he said. "We looked as soon as we got home from The Abbey."

I was embarrassed. But I probably would have done the same, gross factor or not, if I'd found out one of my friends had a sex tape online.

"But don't worry, Malcolm, you done the PBC proud," he said and giggled. Obviously influenced by one too many glasses of sangria. "And for that, I'm sure there's a little freakum dress or nice pair of slutty jeans and a T-shirt and blazer in my closet that you can borrow…from my when-I-was-fat stage."

Chapter 9

Kyle and I were both still hungry when we arrived at the show, even after eating the raw vegetarian feast Bernard left for us. Filling, but unfulfilling.

So the first thing we went for on the massive buffet were the buffalo wings and miniature barbecued ribs.

At the bar, two glasses of wine—white for me, red for Kyle. Didn't want to mix any other types of liquor with our earlier sangrias. Tired *and* a hangover were a no-no for me at work.

We'd just missed the performance by Alice Smith, but still had Chrisette, Dwele, Elle, and Tommie Jordan to go. We found an empty booth/table on the side and rear of the club and raced to sit in it. On our way to the seats, I noticed a few familiar Black singers and actors in the audience, and they were enjoying the fattening appetizers as well as the live DJ spinning old-school R&B in between performers. I was always star-struck whenever I went to one of Kyle's industry events, but was comforted that they, like me, were regular people who liked to eat. So much for the hype that no one eats in L.A. Black people who move to L.A. from other places eat.

"Did you see…" I asked, or started to anyway. "Nothing, forget it."

"Chill, Malcolm," Kyle said. "Yeah, I did."

"I know, my bad," I said.

Part of the façade of Kyle's work world was never to show excitement at being in the company of a celebrity. Somehow, that was seen as a sign of weakness, or that you didn't belong in the circle. The entertainment industry circle. Wearing Kyle's overpriced designer jeans and T-shirt, and being on the guest list, were the only things that put me anywhere close to the same league with the crowd. I couldn't believe I was wearing eight hundred dollars on my back, according to the tags Kyle removed like nothing from the clothes he loaned to me. Although there were a few celebrities in the house, most in attendance were those satellites surrounding the real talent— stylists, producers, talent scouts, publicists, and wannabes.

"So...your nephew," Kyle said, changing the subject. "What are you gonna do with a nineteen-year-old at your house who you're not fucking?"

"Blake's my nephew," I said. "That's kinda not funny, Kyle."

"I know, no disrespect," he said and laughed. I knew what he meant, so no disrespect taken. "But you know you're gonna have to find something for him to do all day."

"I might put Blake to work at LADS," I said. "I haven't spent a lot of time with him since I moved to L.A., so I don't know a lot about his interests other than he's nineteen, gay, and a bit of a troublemaker."

"Well, if I were a nineteen-year-old troublemaker, I don't think I'd be into the charity/LADS thing you do, no offense, unless it's to meet boys," he said.

"Yeah, helping people is boring work," I said. "But somebody's gotta do it."

"Awww, don't get offended, girl. You know what I mean," he said. "Maybe I can find him an internship at the studio, or I'm sure Bernard could use an assistant with the catering company. He has a lot of summer parties to do and could easily pay him."

"We'll see. Blake gets here in a few days."

Kyle looked up over my head. Said under his smile, "Looks like you have a guest. Stay cool."

I felt a tight grip on my right shoulder and turned around to see a belt buckle and a slight hint of a bulge dangling left in my face. Yes, I looked. Then looked up, and saw Tyrell Kincaid smiling down on me.

"Whassup, Mr. Malcolm," he said and gave me a fist bump. "Twice in one day, huh? Never thought you were the type to go out after work."

"Funny how that works out," I said. "This is my buddy Kyle. Kyle, Tyrell."

They shook hands and greeted.

"You look familiar," Tyrell said to Kyle.

"You do, too," Kyle said to Tyrell.

Oh God, I thought. Not the "you look familiar" line gay men use to flirt. Not that I was jealous of Kyle, or that he and Tyrell would hit it off. Besides, Kyle had a man, and Tyrell was not available. What was that jealous moment all about?

Tyrell grabbed my shoulder again and squeezed. As if he were reading my mind. Or just needed me as a place/person to rest his hand on. Squeezed again.

"I didn't think you were into the music thing, man," Tyrell said. "Should be a good show tonight. Alice Smith was dope. You see her?"

"That's what I hear, but we missed her performance," I said. I was star-struck. Tyrell Kincaid, professional basketball player, was having small talk with me. In public. I noticed eyes and heads turning in our direction. I didn't know what else to say, and I didn't want a repeat of the foot-in-mouth moment between Tyrell and me at LADS.

Kyle intervened. Being nosy. "So who are you looking forward to seeing tonight?"

"You know, the whole night is supposed to be good," Tyrell said and turned his attention back to me. "So I'ma get back at you about the lunch or dinner thing, Malcolm. I got paid the big bucks today, Kyle."

Tyrell winked at Kyle and then turned to me. We both smiled, laughed, at the small honorarium I paid him for his talk at LADS. Our own private joke.

"Enjoy the night, guys," Tyrell said before strolling off to greet people at other tables in the club.

"He's a nice guy," I said as I took a longer-than-normal peek at Tyrell walking away. I'd never met a man so tall and massive. My sexually empowered side made a mental note of his broad shoulders, tiny waist, and all that ass, which gave him that perfectly male V-shape, a thought I wouldn't share with Kyle.

"Okaaay," Kyle said and leaned across the table to give me a high five, knocking his red wine across the table with him. Rolled onto my shirt, which was really Kyle's. "Oh my God, I'm sorry."

"It's cool."

"Really. Let me help." Kyle attempted to clean up the spill with a stack of cocktail napkins we'd grabbed to clean our fingers of wings and ribs sauce.

"No problem, it's your clothes anyway," I said and smiled. Kyle smiled with me. "I'ma head to the restroom. Back in a few."

I walked through the crowd until I found a server to direct me to the nearest men's room. Inside, I took off the T-shirt

Kyle had loaned me and ran water over the spot where red wine had spilled on it. Felt a little naked, being dressed in just a tank top, but the attire was similar to some of the guys sitting in the club or playing onstage. Only thing, a thirty-five-year old doesn't carry a tank top the same way as a man of twenty-five. Gave me better incentive to get out as much of the wine stain as possible.

The men's room door opened, and a trendy-dressed young man walked through. I heard him whisper a "whassup" as he walked to the urinal a few feet to my left. I continued working on my shirt until it looked presentable enough for public viewing.

"Whassup," the young man said as he stood behind me in the mirror.

"I'm sorry. I'll be out of your way. Spilled something on my shirt."

"It's cool, man," he said and grinned. He moved a little closer to me. "Kinda digging the view from right here."

"I beg your pardon," I said. I wanted to add "young man," but didn't. I could see I was older than he, but didn't feel he deserved a respectful modifier.

"I thought I saw you checking me out in the mirror," he said. "That's all."

I ignored him. Moved out of his way and a little to the right to put my shirt under the blow-dryer.

"I saw your video, yo," he said and put a hand over his zipper. "Man, you know how to suck a dick."

"Excuse me?"

"Your videos. I saw a bunch of 'em online, actually," he said. "Couldn't believe it when I saw you walk in the club tonight. You're like the male Superhead."

"I don't know what you're talking about," I said, even

though I knew *exactly* what he was talking about. "Wrong guy here."

"It's cool if you wanna be discreet and all," he said and handed me a business card. An independent publicist / producer, no company affiliation. In L.A., that meant you just moved here and didn't have a real job. "I got a girl who keeps me broke off good, but I like to get down every now and then, if you know what I mean. Like you did in the video."

"Um, okay."

I left, not making any more small talk with the young music producer, nor making a deal to get down with him.

When I returned to the table, Kyle was nursing a new glass of red wine. I knew it would be a while before we'd leave. He drove a stick and I left my keys at his and Bernard's house.

"What took you so long?" Kyle asked. "It's a hundred-dollar throwaway. And you missed Tyrell, who came back looking for you again. Someone's 'bout to get dicked down by the ball player."

"Kyle, please, you're buzzing," I said. "You'll never guess what happened in the bathroom."

"Better than Tyrell Kincaid?"

"Nothing like that," I said and leaned in toward Kyle to whisper. "Someone else saw those videos. He propositioned me."

"Are you serious? Is he still here? Do you wanna go?"

"Yes. Yes. And yes. But I know you can't drive yet," I said. "I'll just chill until you're ready."

"Was he cute?" Kyle said. "I mean…"

"Now, Kyle," I said. A little disappointed that his first response would be to inquire about the guy's looks.

"I'm sorry, Malcolm. That sucks."

"Yeah, it sucks," I said. "I could kill Deacon for what he did."

We stayed silent for a few seconds. I was thinking. I'm sure Kyle was thinking of what to say to console me.

"I mean, if two random strangers saw those videos and then me in public," I said and continued, "how long before someone I *know* sees them?"

CHAPTER 10

I didn't have to wait too long.

The next morning when I arrived at the center, DeMarco said I'd had five urgent messages from the LADS Board of Directors co-chair, two from the office of the local city council representative, and one from the youth minister of the church a few blocks away, who was one of the more vocal board members. I was already cranky because it was eighty degrees already at eight thirty in the morning. Hot. Late June. Urgent messages. Plus tired from the music showcase last night, which ended at three in the morning. Not a winning combination.

"My God, DeMarco," I said and sighed. "Did they say what they wanted?"

"They said it's about some video or something," DeMarco said. "You know anything about a video?"

It was obvious that DeMarco's new boyfriend, Compton, hadn't said anything about me or seeing me on GayClick. Or it wasn't Compton who I'd seen picking up DeMarco yesterday after work. Or maybe DeMarco was just helping me save face by not letting me know he knew about the videos Deacon leaked. Whatever scenario, it didn't matter. The people who mattered had seen the videos, obviously.

"Let me take the messages," I said and grabbed the

message cards from DeMarco. "I'll be on the phone for a while this morning, so unless it's the board president..."

"Gotcha, boss," DeMarco said and winked. At least he didn't have on those damn sunglasses at the front desk again. "Let me know if you need anything."

I heard hip-hop music playing from the desktop, but given the circumstances, decided it wasn't so urgent to reprimand DeMarco.

"I'll let you know," I said.

"And I'll get offline," he said. "I was adding friends from my page to the LADS page."

"Whatever, DeMarco," I said. I probably rolled my eyes or responded flippantly, but wasn't too caring about how I came across. "Just hold down the fort up front. And if anyone, and I mean *anyone*, asks you anything related to the organization or me, don't answer anything. Even if it's the normal spiel you give to people inquiring about LADS."

"Yes, boss."

"Come to think of it..." I said, as I contemplated closing down the office for the day. "Never mind. Just hold it down for me. I'll update you in a few."

Little did I know that those few minutes would turn into hours.

CHAPTER 11

I hated the kind of meetings where you knew the agenda of the person running it was set, and the decisions were already made, and your feedback was just hot air. I always saw them as a waste of time, as there was nothing to do other than agree to whatever the chair wanted or set forth.

The LADS Board of Directors called an emergency meeting that afternoon. The meeting was no different than the kind I hated. Despite the fact that most, if not all, of the members had a day job or other obligations, there was a quorum to make the meeting legal and on the books, a requirement for agencies like LADS to stay chartered with the city and neighborhood council.

I knew it was starting in the wrong direction when Lamont Murphy, the board member who happened to be a youth minister for the church two blocks from LADS, chimed in.

"So you're teaching the young men here how to do pornography?" Lamont said, after barely leafing through the information packet I'd prepared for the meeting, just in case the board members wanted a reminder of the good work I'd done running LADS and for the young men using the services. He'd tossed it aside, seemingly assured that he wouldn't learn anything new from it. "Isn't that kind of stereotypical for the community of young men and boys you work with?"

Men like Lamont Murphy made me sick. Further, it was ironic that a man like Lamont Murphy could talk about stereotypes, as he was a walking one. As usual, he wore a too-tight black suit in the middle of the ninety-degree afternoon, and his processed hair was reminiscent of Barry White. The only thing youthful about him was that his hair and suit were trendy around Barry White's heyday in the seventies. Sad, because Lamont Murphy was probably just a year or two older than me. Obviously trying to fit in with the elder ministers he aspired to assume leadership from in the future.

"Nothing could be further from the truth, Pastor Murphy," I said.

"Well, I'd say your actions definitely match the first objective of the LADS curriculum," he said and pointed to the cover sheet of the packet I'd prepared.

On it, I'd included the main objectives of LADS and what I'd hope it would accomplish with the organization. Reverend Murphy had chosen to focus on point one: LADS clients will learn to make smart and sexually empowered decisions for their lives and health.

"What exactly is 'smart and sexually empowered'?" Reverend Murphy asked, with his brows furrowed and eyes squinted at me. "Is that what you'd call making a series of pornographic videos like you did?"

I paused and took a breath. I thought about Kyle's advice he'd shared when I got a moment of his time in between returning messages.

"Just tell them the truth," Kyle said. Though I didn't have the money to retain him as my attorney, though I didn't think I needed one, Kyle always was willing to share his legal opinions on whatever I asked him. "Don't make up lies or try to 'politician' your way out of it. But if you need me to come over there for support or counsel, I will."

I chose not to have Kyle leave his day at the studio, and now, as I had to answer sensitive questions about my personal life—my personal sex life and relationship with Deacon—I wish I'd taken Kyle up on his offer. I wished I'd called Deacon over to explain what he'd done, but considering what I did to his laptop, I'm sure coming to my defense was the last thing on his mind.

"Reverend Murphy…members of the board," I said and looked around the table, making sure I caught each one in the eye, "I don't teach the young men here anything inappropriate. I try to empower each of them with the skills they'll need so they won't be a statistic or a stereotype. And if they happen to be a stereotype, so what? We're not trying to create clones that are safe for straight people or the mainstream, white LGBT community. But that's not the point. What's important is that before I opened up LADS, there were very few to no community organizations focused primarily on young, gay African American men in Los Angeles. Through the services and resources offered the past two years, we've been able to help almost forty young men find jobs in areas they want to work in. Our numbers of new HIV infections are at or below the city's and county's average, and well below organizations focused on young, gay men of other ethnicities of color. The education efforts are working, and the pre and post LADS awareness numbers show the young men are learning how to prevent HIV infections. All of that you can see in the information packets I've shared."

"But what does that have to do with the pornography you made?" Reverend Murphy asked. I wondered why he was so fascinated, and why he had a fascination with the word "pornography." "What does sexual empowerment have to do with pornography and young Black men?"

I looked around the table at the rest of the board members,

wondering why none was coming to my defense. I thought I knew the board members. I'd selected or at least had a hand in selecting most of them to participate, except for the city councilperson's assistant and Reverend Lamont Murphy.

"It might have looked like pornography, but it wasn't," I said. "I was in a committed and loving relationship at the time, and those videos you saw were of him and me while we were together many years ago. I never knew I was being videotaped."

"Really?" Finally, another board member spoke up, though his voice had a tinge of sarcasm in it. "We're supposed to believe that in not one, not two, but more than fifty times of having sex with your boyfriend, you never noticed a camera in the room?"

"You won't believe me, but no."

"A boyfriend you were committed to? Whose house you'd been to on numerous occasions?"

"People do duplicitous things, I've come to learn," I said. "Deacon has done the most disgusting thing and betrayed my trust by videotaping our most private moments. We're not even together anymore."

"Then who put them on the Internet for the whole world to see?" Reverend Murphy chimed in again. "If you two were so in love, as you would lead us to believe, then why would he betray you like that? What did you do to make him so angry that he would put your sex life online, knowing the work you do? It's one thing to not know you were videotaped, as you say you did not. It's another to put that pornography online for our youth and the boys you serve at LADS to see."

The meeting seemed to go nowhere, and everywhere, fast. Then came the barrage of questions that I didn't think I deserved, nor ever expected to face. Not Malcolm, the good boy.

"What about your reputation, Malcolm?"

"How do you think this will damage the boys?"

"What makes you any different than a porn star?"

"How can you educate and be a professional role model with these kinds of videos floating around of you?"

"Are you Black first, or gay first?" That was out of nowhere.

The board members continued to ask me, and each other, questions about me, the videos, the mission of LADS, and what I thought would happen when the videos made the rounds on the Internet and in the Black community. The last question, about being a professional role model, stung the most. I thought, if *they* forgave R. Kelly, someone who only made music, the Black community would forgive me, someone who was doing something to make a positive difference with young men no one wanted to acknowledge in the community. It all seemed like a blur. And the meeting had definitely gotten out of my control, which was unusual for me. In times of crisis, I knew how to dig in, put on my poker face, and talk people to my way of thinking. Some called it posturing. I called it surviving as a smart and empowered Black man in the late 2000s. This time, though, pulling what I called a Hillary was not working. Maybe I needed to pull a Barack, or better yet, a Michelle from South Side Chicago to make sure they *knew* who they were dealing with.

In between questions, I'd started doing the mental math on my personal finances and budget. What I *wanted* to get by on, and what I *needed* to survive. Those moments, I liked to say, were when God, or my late father, were speaking to me and guiding my thoughts.

"You know what," I said and handed over a piece of paper to the board chair. "I'm the one who works day to day with the young men who use LADS. You all just come in once a quarter to get reports to take back to your constituents…to say you care about Black queer folks, and HIV and AIDS education. But that's okay. I'm going to be okay. LADS is going to be okay."

"And we've appreciated your work, Malcolm," Reverend Murphy said. "I always speak highly of what you've…"

"Whatever, sure you have," I said, feeling myself getting tense and defensive. Definitely not professional demeanor, but the board members were far from professional with me. "You all can't even get a consortium of people to make Black gay pride happen consistently in L.A. and most major cities, and you're worried about some sex tapes between consensual adults."

"At least I don't suck dick like a prostitute," Reverend Murphy said. He slammed his hand on the table for emphasis as he scooted away from the table. "Smart and sexually empowered, my ass."

"Spoken like a true Sunday-morning sermon," I said. "You act like you've never made a mistake before."

"I make…I've made mistakes."

"When? In 1992?"

I heard a chuckle from someone at the table, but didn't look to see who found me a little funny in responding to the reverend. Glad I didn't. I probably would have lost it and laughed too.

"We need order in this meeting, my brothers." The board chair spoke up and looked at the paper I'd handed him. "What's this number? Does this have to do with the number of hits your videos have gotten on the Internet?"

"It's my price to resign."

"LADS doesn't have this kind of money," Reverend Murphy said once he took a look at my request, which the board chair had passed around the table. "The low six figures.

Why don't you sell those videos you're producing online to make some extra spending cash?"

"Not funny, Lamont," I said. I didn't care at that point if I was calling him out of his title or name. I wanted to add that I was sure he and his wife would be the first customers to download my videos, but figured that would be unnecessary gasoline on the flames. "Actually, if you'd done your homework and looked further in the report, LADS is in good shape in terms of a contingency fund, reserves, and investments. Pay me from reserves."

"That's quite a sum."

"It's what I put into LADS initially," I said. "If I leave the organization, I want what I put into it so I can start a new life. The rest is six months of what would have been my salary as Executive Director of LADS. It's a tough economy out there to be looking for work."

I needed my initial investment in LADS in order to survive. I wanted six months of salary to figure out what I'd do with my life.

In the end, I got what I needed *and* wanted.

The board got my letter of resignation by eight o'clock that evening.

CHAPTER 12

For the first time since I was fifteen, I was without a job.
I'd pulled out all my spiral notebooks that had served
as personal journals and diaries since I was a high school
freshman. Fourteen years old when I started. Still keeping
them at age thirty-five.

Since my nephew Blake would be arriving in L.A. in a
few days, I knew I'd have to straighten up the second bedroom
in my apartment. It had been serving as an office, Kyle's or a
boyfriend's friend hangover-can't-drive room, and study space
since I'd moved in almost ten years earlier.

To feel somewhat productive about the cleaning process, I
started with the boxes of journals, which had been sitting on the
sleeper sofa in the room. I thought I'd just move the boxes into
the closet in my bedroom, but nostalgia got the best of me, and
I pulled out my ninth-going-into-tenth grade journal. Fifteen
years old. The summer I got my first job. A peer counselor for
a sex-education program through the local Catholic parish in
Indianapolis. Sex, sexuality, education, and morals had been
with me for too long. It was time for a change.

I pulled my current journal from the bookcase and hit the
Shuffle button on my iTunes. Sat back in the middle of the
floor with a box of my life's recollections.

I couldn't believe I'd been in the same apartment for
the ten years I'd lived in L.A. Certainly by now, and with

my past experience in banking, I would and could have owned something. Even if it was a shack, in the middle of a neighborhood that resembled a shooting gallery with police helicopters that circled overhead all day.

Times like this I tried not to compare my life to Kyle. True, he'd gone on to law school—UCLA—after our Northwestern University days, while I settled for *just* the four-year bachelor's degree. True, Kyle treated his dating life like an upwardly mobile career track, while I likened my dating life to social work—if the man had problems, I felt sorry for, thought I could save, was attracted to, and dated him. Definitely not the kind of role modeling and example I should have been setting for the guys at LADS. A pattern of dating people you feel sorry for is just plain sad and sorry. If I'd had a glass of wine, I'd have been on a downward slide to a depression session. Without a buzz, I was just reflective and thinking about the circle of life, what I'd created and what I'd been dealt. And that sucked.

With the check I'd be getting from the LADS Board of Directors, I could put a healthy down payment on a home, maybe a small town house or condo in Inglewood or Leimert Park that was being foreclosed. Finally put some roots down in L.A. for myself and Blake, if he chose to stay beyond the summer. But with no current job, I'd have to think about making the monthly mortgage payment. A lump sum would only go so far, even in a recovering real estate market in Southern California.

I put the journal aside and lay in the middle of the floor. There were a couple more days to clean and prepare for Blake's arrival. I turned up the music and wondered if it was a sign from above that Shirley Horn's "Where Do You Start?" had just started playing on my iTunes.

It made me wonder. What does an unemployed thirty-five year old Black gay man start when life as he knows it is over?

CHAPTER 13

That night, I dreamed that I was slipping on ice.

I wasn't quite sure if it was an ice rink or an ice pond. But every time I tried to walk to the edge, to solid ground, I kept slipping and sliding across the ice.

The dream happened more than once throughout the night.

When I woke up in the morning, it looked like someone had ransacked my apartment. Books were strewn around and on me, where I'd fallen asleep in the middle of the floor. The sofa was askew and a few inches out from the wall. But nothing looked to be missing.

I reached for the remote control to turn on the television. After a few minutes of resetting channels, it settled on the local CBS affiliate and the morning news.

I learned I'd slept through a series of moderate earthquakes in the middle of the night.

CHAPTER 14

I had ten voicemail and seven text messages when cell phone service was finally restored. Most were from out-of-town people wondering if I'd survived my first real earthquakes in Los Angeles. It was a subject for which I had no real response, because I'd slept through most of the night's activity.

"Lord have mercy," my sister Marlena said when we finally connected. "There's no way I could deal. But of course DUMB-ASS BLAKE is eager and ready for earthquake country."

"Marlena," I said. "Stop arguing with him. Is he there?"

"He's got on those goddamn iPod headphones again, he can't hear me," she said. "I'm dropping him off at the airport early. He couldn't wait to get out to L.A. And oh, did I tell you I FOUND A LITTLE WHITE BOY SNEAKING OUT HIS ROOM when I got home from work this morning. A WHITE BOY. You know what mama used to tell us. Anybody but a white boy. Ain't no white boys living around here, so I know he probably met him on that damn Internet again."

I sighed. The trials and tribulations of Marlena and Blake Campbell.

"You're dropping him off at the airport now? Today?"

"Praise the Lord," she said. "Now me and the girls can have a peaceful summer."

"We just had an earthquake, Marlena," I said. "I don't even know how the freeways are. Or if LAX is open." Everything *was* fine, according to the news. I was just trying to stall Blake's inevitable arrival.

"You talking to me, right?" she asked. "If phone lines are up, then everything is okay."

I could tell she was just eager for Blake to be gone. Be damned if I could accommodate him today.

"Whatever. Thanks for the warning."

"You didn't even ask me about the GODDAMN WHITE BOY COMING OUT OF BLAKE'S ROOM," she yelled, again to get Blake's attention as, I'm sure, he enjoyed ignoring my sister in the car. "One of those pale ones with eyeliner, and all kinds of piercings, and black eyeliner and lipstick…I thought the gays had taste and…"

"All right, Marlena. I appreciate the call. Text me the landing time and I'll be there," I said. "Landlord is here to look at the apartment for earthquake damage."

I hung up and panicked. The room I'd started preparing for Blake was nowhere near ready. But I figured that a nineteen-year-old wouldn't really care how ready a room was, as long as there was music, a computer, and something to lie back and sleep on. Still, I'd have to get those books that fell on and around me off the floor, and do a lazy cleanup job—shove things under or in locations not seen to the naked eye—for the rest of what would soon be Blake's room.

Kyle called and I picked up on the second ring.

"Girl, you're alive. Thanks for calling your sista," Kyle said.

"My apologies," I said. "I just got off the phone with my *real* sister. My nephew's coming today instead of later in the week."

"Lucky you. Yum."

"That's my nephew," I said, grossed out that Kyle was teasing about Blake that way. "Anyway, I'm cleaning up his room now. How's your place?"

"We felt all the quakes," Kyle said and giggled. "Then made a few of our own. It was kinda hot. But no damage to the house, believe it or not."

"No damage here, either. I slept through everything."

"You *would*," Kyle said. "One was almost six-point. The others were in the four and five range."

"I hate it. My first real California quakes. Though I did have a dream I was slipping and falling on ice. Maybe that was a sign."

"Boring," Kyle said. "So, girl, I guess you haven't heard. Well, no, you wouldn't because you don't work in entertainment. Well, you don't work either."

"Whatever."

"We got the advance view of tonight's *Paparazzi Players* show, and you'll never guess who got caught in a gay sex club, on video, before and after the earthquake?"

"Who?"

"You better sit down, stretch, and get ready for your man."

"Huh?"

"Tommie Jordan, the self-proclaimed emperor of R&B."

"No way," I said.

"Way."

"A sex club?"

"Yes, as in a private club where men pay to hook up with other men," Kyle said. "As in a bathhouse. As in where closeted men go for a few discreet dalliances while their wives think they're out watching the game with the fellas."

"I get it, Kyle," I said. "But why a sex club? Can't he get it whenever he wants? I mean, Tommie Jordan's a celebrity."

"That's what I said, girl," Kyle said.

"So what happened?"

"I guess one of the faults from last night's quake runs through West Hollywood, and it damaged the sex club where Tommie was at," Kyle said. "So they had to send rescue crews to get these poor queens off the second floor of this place, since the stairs had sorta collapsed, come undone. And of course the cameras just happened to be there when Tommie Jordan walked out with the help of a firefighter assigned to help."

"And isn't he with Tyrell, supposedly? Why would he cheat on a basketball player of all people?"

"Maybe Tyrell don't bring in the gold, who knows?" Kyle said. "Of course *Paparazzi Players* can't show all the *nasty* nasty, but if you get Internet now you might find some of the pics or videos. You know how the boy-girls are with their celebrity gossip and the Internet."

"Yeah, I *know*."

"Oh, shoot, of course you do."

"Whatevers, Kyle."

"So I think you might wanna give Mr. Tyrell Kincaid a call once all the *ish* hits the fan…show him some of your outreach and empathy skills."

"You're funny, Kyle," I said. "No way Tyrell would even think of calling on me after knowing each other for a couple days. And how do they know this video is true of Tommie?"

"Girl, believe me, it's true," Kyle said. "I saw all of Tommie Jordan in the flesh letting some young guy sing to the mike. But the legitimate news video shows him walking out of the place with the help of a rescue worker. Can't deny he was coming out of a sex club. He might deny the other stuff posted by the queens who serviced him, though."

"That's just unbelievable."

"Not really…even *you* were in a video, Malcolm," he said. "What could be stranger than that?"

CHAPTER 15

S omething stranger did happen.

About fifteen minutes after I got off the phone with Kyle, there was a knock at my apartment door. I wasn't expecting any guests other than Blake and maybe the landlord to inspect for any potential earthquake damage. As for Blake, I knew it was too early and he wasn't smart enough to figure a way to get my place from the airport. I looked at the clock. Just after ten in the morning.

"Surprise."

Tyrell Kincaid was standing at my door, scrunched just a little to appear under the door frame.

"How did you know where I lived?" I asked. "What are you doing here?"

"I'm famous. I can find out anything if the price is right," he said.

"Okay." Seemed a little weird for Tyrell to research my address and show up at my place. Out of the blue. I thought the stalking was supposed to happen the other way around.

"Actually, I was just out in the neighborhood and assessing all the earthquake damage…thought I'd check in on you," he said. Paused. "Actually, believe it or not, I don't have a lot of friends and thought maybe I could come by. And I wanted to make sure you were okay."

"Come in," I said. "But excuse the mess. I'm still cleaning up a bit. Just a few books on the floor and two broken dishes. Could have been worse, huh?"

Tyrell looked around my apartment. I was embarrassed a little. Even with the minor disarray from the earthquake, my home was nicely decorated and suitable for me as a single, formerly hardworking person. I didn't need much. But it was nice, and except for what would be Blake's room, clean. Still, I could only imagine the kinds of plush and ornate things Tyrell surrounded himself at his house...houses, if I remembered the background information correctly.

"Cool place," he said. "I remember my first place when I was in college."

"Oh, so you're saying I live like a college student?" I smiled and he laughed.

"Not at all, Malcolm," he said. "It's nice. Simple. No complications. I can't believe my life was like that at one time. Mind if I have a seat?"

I removed some old *Clik* magazines I'd taken from Blake's room to make room for Tyrell and me to sit on the sofa. Why I was keeping old issues of the magazine was beyond belief, unless I was planning to audition for that TV show *Hoarders*.

"Go ahead, help yourself," I said. "Want something to drink? I've got orange juice, soy milk, or water."

He sat. "Got some whiskey?"

I stared at Tyrell. He wasn't laughing or being light-hearted at what would typically be a fun gay suggestion of drinking cocktails at ten in the morning.

"Okay, what's up?" I asked and sat on the other end of the sofa.

I remembered my conversation with Kyle a few minutes earlier, so I knew what was up before the rest of the world would. I just couldn't let on that I knew, and could only respond to what Tyrell chose to share in his own time.

"It's long and complicated," Tyrell said. "I feel like drinking and I don't drink, Malcolm. I just thought I could talk to you. I used to be able to talk to my dad about these things, but since he passed..."

"Of course."

"I don't even know you that well," he said. "I don't really trust the people around me anymore. So I'm trusting you and talking to you because I feel like we kinda connected after I spoke at LADS the other day."

I was listening, but not listening, but listening to Tyrell Kincaid. I was more listening to myself and my mind chatter: *there's a professional basketball player sitting in my living room*; *he's trusting me with his personal life*; *he's so damn attractive*; *there's a millionaire professional basketball player sitting in my living room; he's confiding in me*; *there's a famous person talking to non-famous ME, person-to-person.*

"...so then he comes home this morning after all the quakes and tells me what I'm going to be seeing on the tabloid shows tonight," Tyrell said. "Just like nothing. Just like he was telling me that he was buying new underwear, going to the movies, or something."

"I bet you were shocked." Typical, non-emotional counseling voice. In my mind thinking, *He just came out to me... Tyrell Kincaid, professional basketball player, just confirmed what the world has been speculating... to ME.*

"Kind of but not really," he said. "Tommie's done this for years... well, the cheating part. We've got so many people on payroll who we're paying to keep silent, it's pitiful. The sex in public thing at sex clubs and sex parties. *That's* new. I'm such a fool, you know? You'd think I'd have a little more pride than I do."

"It's understandable that you would question yourself when you feel his choices reflect on you."

"I should leave him," Tyrell said. "I've almost left him over a dozen times. But something always keeps me running back. Hard to trust people…dudes in the life…when you're a public figure, you know. Even in these times. So I just stay."

"I know it can be difficult to end something you see as being special."

I thought of Deacon for a moment. Leaving him when I did was the best thing I did, but it hurt. I knew it would have been worse to stay and not be supported in my dreams. I would have left him sooner had I known about his little camera hobby.

"Things with Tommie and me used to be special, like when we first met all those years ago when I was playing at UCLA and he hadn't made his big music comeback and was just working in a CD store…when we *had* CD stores," he said and smiled. "Then Rafael came along—the bitch— and started doing Tommie while I traveled with the team. We were all in the same circle at the time…me, this guy named Keith who was Tommie's roommate, some other guy, Marco, I don't really remember. Whatever, that's all ancient history. But the cheating never stopped. Even when he said it would. He'd always pull that 'it was just physical, not love like we have.'"

"Just physical, not love," I said and sighed. Perpetual cheaters and their predictability. Innocent victims and our gullibility. "I've heard that before. But this is not about me."

We sat on our respective ends of the sofa in silence. I knew that if and when Tyrell wanted to talk more, he would. I wouldn't push.

"So I'm going to be the laughingstock of the basketball league and of the Black celebrity world," Tyrell said. "Figures.

It's funny and sad. As if they don't know about us. The whole world's been speculating about us forever. I'm not naïve to the gossip."

"I don't know how Black celebrity works, but it sounds like it's important to you."

"Tommie never wanted to be out, so to speak," Tyrell said. "Even when those activists outed me, tried to out me, with that information they got from someone in my circle, Tommie wanted me to deny everything about me and us. So I just played nonchalant and like I have been dateless and sexless since birth. Like I wasn't gay or with anyone. That allowed Tommie to do whatever he wanted. I'll have that juice now, changing the subject. Whatever you have to mix in it is fine."

"Sounds good," I said and stood up. "Keep talking. I'm listening."

I walked to the kitchen, where I began pouring glasses of juice. Just juice, no liquor. Started to prepare fruit slices, cheese, and wheat crackers, but decided it seemed too *As The World Turns* to have a tray of food for our talk. Instead grabbed a couple of bananas and napkins, and then went back to the living room.

Tyrell was stretched out across my sofa and his eyes were closed. His legs dangled for several feet off the end. He looked like a big kid napping in my living room. I grabbed the blanket from what would become Blake's room and stretched it across Tyrell.

"I'ma just rest my eyes for a minute." Tyrell sighed and pulled the blanket up to his chin. "Hope you don't mind."

As if I would say no to a pro basketball player who wanted to sleep in my living room and on my sofa.

"Oh," he said. "Thanks for listening. I knew I could turn to you."

"No problem, Tyrell," I said.

"Would you lay with me?" Tyrell said. "Cuddle with me?"

Everyone and their grandma would have said "hell yeah" to a request from a pro basketball player. But I'd just met him. He was vulnerable. I didn't want to be turned and tossed out, like any number of conquests pro athletes seemed to have at their disposal. He couldn't possibly want to cuddle with *me*. Not Malcolm Martin Campbell, ordinary, respectable Black guy, no labels, no title, from Indiana living in L.A.

"Anytime but now, Tyrell," I said. "My nephew's coming to L.A. later today. I'm trying to fix his room. So much to…"

"I understand," Tyrell said and closed his eyes. "Next time."

I wondered if there'd be a next time with someone like Tyrell Kincaid, as I cleaned and he napped. Even though we were barely getting to know each other, I hoped there would be a next time. Certainly, no one turned down a celebrity request, but it wasn't every day that your nephew was moving in with you either.

CHAPTER 16

Tyrell's minute-long nap turned into a couple hours.

In that time, I'd finished Blake's room and had started making dinner for us to eat after I picked him up from the airport. I remembered from times when I'd gone back to Indianapolis for holidays or family reunions that Blake had a favorite meal—fried turkey chops (but sitting in foil for a few hours, not directly out of the skillet), creamed corn, and applesauce. I'd done my best to make it as close to what my mother or my sister Marlena would make, and Blake would just have to enjoy my attempt.

In between flouring turkey chops, I turned on the television anchored just below the kitchen cabinets. Wanted to see if any of the news Kyle or Tyrell had shared had become public. I flipped to *The Livonia Birmingham Show*, with a host who prided herself on having the latest gossip and gossipy opinions, especially when it came to insinuating a celebrity might be gay.

"So at the gym the other day, Livonia Birmingham ran into one-hit-wonder and one-time R&B diva-in-training Peaches Perkins, who was training...not with her personal trainer for her body, but with gym management for a new job as an aerobics instructor...oops, I mean hip-hop class choreographer. Seems that Miss Peaches, who's now crack-

free, weave-free, and ass-free thanks to a major diet and detox process, is proud of her changes and says she may have found Mr. Right in one of her three Twelve Step groups she attends faithfully. Go girl! Make your changes! Gives us something to look forward to when you backslide...psych! We loves Miss Peaches, and hope she can make a comeback like some R&B male singers have been given a chance to do.

"Speaking of comebacks, I hate outing those who are not out, but when Livonia Birmingham gets a hint of a tip, Livonia Birmingham sure is going to follow up. All I can say is dribble the ball and put the mike to your mouth. Yum! This will make HUGE news later today, but let's just say I don't foresee this super-hyper-masculine duo to be waving the Proud 'Nuff to Come Out flag like Lance Bass or Sheryl Swoopes did a few years back. Tight-lipped publicists. Maybe if one of the duo was a little tighter-lipped, the other wouldn't step out and about with the young, hung, and restless thugalicious fans of his work and body. That's another story, another day. If you got video of any special interactions with a celebrity, hit me up...and you're PAID!"

I flipped to the afternoon edition of *Paparazzi Players.* The show led with the footage of Tommie Jordan trying to cover his face with a magazine while leaving the sex club— footage I'm sure *The Livonia Birmingham Show* wanted first. The reporter softened the blow for the afternoon audience by calling it a men's spa. Tommie refused comment. The paparazzi made several offensive comments trying to goad Tommie into talking—*How many fans you got in the spa? Does your basketball player boyfriend mind you being a swinger? Do you and Tyrell throw sex parties at your mansion?* From the number of cameras swirling around Tommie Jordan, one would think Black celebrities were equally in demand as white celebrities by the entertainment media. And then I thought, with all the poverty, hunger, and violence plaguing parts of Los Angeles, why was the public/private sex life of a celebrity such a big deal? I mean in comparison. Kind of like how the Black gay organizations couldn't pull off Black Prides in various parts of the country, yet the board of my organization was more concerned with my private sex life.

The story continued with several seconds of footage featuring Tommie Jordan receiving attention and being serviced by numerous men of different ethnicities, ages, and sizes inside the club. Some was too raw for the afternoon audience and featured blacked-out sections of the screen. Apparently, someone carried a small, unnoticeable camera or phone and shot numerous scenes of Tommie having sex, undetected. I knew I could call Kyle to find the raw footage online or could wait until after midnight for *Paparazzi Players Uncut* on cable.

"Something smells so good, Malcolm, it woke me up," Tyrell said and appeared in the doorway of the kitchen. He looked at the television playing on the countertop. "Damn, they're running the story about Tommic."

"That's not the worse of it," I said and shut off *Paparazzi Players*. "They're looking for you now, and I'm sure they won't stop until they get answers."

CHAPTER 17

I can't believe you wanted to come with me to LAX," I said. "Thanks…I guess."

I was riding in Tyrell's truck, a cream-colored Lexus with standard state-issued plates, heading west on the super-crowded 105 greeway toward the airport. Luckily, we cruised in the carpool lane with ease.

This was Tyrell's hideaway car, the one he drove when he just wanted to be a regular, everyday person. I sank in the plush leather passenger seat while we flipped satellite television stations looking for anything on Tommie or Tyrell. Other than the early pieces on *Livonia Birmingham* or *Paparazzi Players*, the bulk of the news would hit television in the evening entertainment shows.

"I wanted to give your nephew something to talk about," he said as he looked ahead on the road. Then he cracked a smile. "I mean, if you're going to do L.A., do it big, huh?"

"Whatever," I said. "You're crazy."

"You're crazy."

"No, you showing up and hiding out at my little Silver Lake apartment avoiding paparazzi is crazy," I said. "You going to the airport to pick up my nephew—a crazy situation in itself—is crazy. You hanging out with me, someone you don't even know…and you're famous…is crazy."

He smiled again. I rolled my eyes and thought about the craziness of it all. Less than a week ago, I'd barely met Tyrell Kincaid. Twenty-four hours earlier, I was fired by the board of LADS. For the past six hours I'd been hanging with and hiding out a professional basketball player who was embroiled in his own hot, gay, and closeted mess. Kyle, and everyone else who knew me, would definitely think the situation was crazy. Or, at minimum, unreal. I was with someone famous.

"I'm just Tyrell," he said. "The only difference is that way more people know me than you. But your work is *way* more important than mine. I dig that."

"That's a cool way of putting it, I guess."

"I hope you think I'm cool."

I didn't think I'd heard him right. "What?"

"Huh?" Tyrell said.

"You said something?"

"Nah," he said and smiled. "I don't know how long this will take to blow over, if ever, but I know for sure I'm through with Tommie Jordan. I might be through with the whole closet thing too."

"Really?"

"What has it gotten me?"

"Well, duh, millions of dollars by playing the role," I said. I hadn't meant to mention any of Tyrell's money. It was the last thing on my mind in terms of our…friendship…and I didn't want him thinking I was like any other person who suddenly found him or herself in the same orbit with a celebrity—unknown motives. "That came out wrong, Tyrell. You got to have a career that many young boys dream of, is what I meant to say. Pro ball. That's all because of God, and definitely possible because you stayed in the closet, performing gender."

"Yeah," he said and cracked that million-dollar smile again. "I know you're not a gold digger, Malcolm."

"Not at all."

"I just hope you can be patient. You're patient, right?"

"Huh?" I said, playing the same game he'd played on me a few seconds earlier.

"What?" He was looking out the side of his right eye at me, I could see, as he spoke.

"You said something about patience, Tyrell?"

"Nah," he said and grinned. "Just enjoy the ride. Enjoy the scenery of Inglewood. We're about to give your nephew the surprise of his life."

CHAPTER 18

When we pulled into the lane for Arrivals, there was little traffic. I anticipated an easy time getting in and out of the airport once we got Blake from the baggage claim of Delta Airlines. I called Blake once and got his voicemail. On the second try, he answered.

"What up, Unc?" Blake said. "I just got my first bag and waiting on my second."

"Good deal," I said. "I'm pulling up to the baggage area. A friend drove me, so we'll pull over and I'll come in to help you. Is it crowded?"

"Nah, just feel like I'm in Hollywood already," he said. "I think they're filming a movie or something. I'm 'bout to be famous, Unc!"

"See you in a few. You remember how I look?"

"Of course. You remember me, your favorite nephew, don't you?"

"I only have one."

I hung up. Tyrell told me he'd pull up and wait for me to get Blake. Said he'd flatter a couple of the traffic cops with autographs and casual conversation, which would allow him to sit a few extra minutes in the restricted pickup zone.

Tyrell zoomed into a spot that had just opened outside the sliding doors of Delta. I jumped out and headed toward the baggage claim carousel. As predicted, a couple of traffic cops thinking he was just a regular L.A. resident went to Tyrell's driver-side window, which he'd begun to lower. I could see him flashing his smile and initiating the conversation with the cops, who were clearly awed that they were speaking with a professional basketball player. No yelling or warning a celebrity they'd be towed for waiting outside baggage claim. So L.A. to cater to celebrity.

I kept walking into the claim area and saw Blake standing at the baggage turnstile. My nephew was handsomer than I'd remembered. Though I'd known Blake all his life, he was two years old when I moved from Indianapolis to Chicago to attend Northwestern. Seeing him on breaks during his toddler years, then maybe once every year or two after that when I moved to California, I hadn't quite gotten the picture of what a hottie he'd turned out to be. I could see how he could be a head-turner to all those young men back in Indiana that my sister complained about.

Just over six feet tall, he was dressed in a fitted white T-shirt, an open black blazer, and low-hung jeans that fit in all the right places. The oversized nerd glasses and multicolored sneakers added the right touch to the look. Real L.A. trendy for a young man just off the plane from the Midwest. It was a shame he hadn't channeled all that creative energy he spent on clothes and anonymous sex on something more productive like higher education after high school. I guess that was part of Marlena's reason for shipping him to me for the summer.

"Blake," I called as I approached and tapped his shoulder. He was clearly concentrating on the baggage and the music blasting from his iPod headphones. "Hey."

He turned, and once it registered who I was, he smiled and pulled out one earbud.

"What up, Uncle Malcolm?"

We hugged. His lean skeletal build shocked me at first touch. The magic of nineteen. Older men had more cushion and meat with their hugs. I'd have to do a major L.A. diet to reach my high school weight and body again, but I wasn't a fan of eating disorders.

"Not much," I said. "Just waiting on you, Blake. Is this your bag?"

"Yeah," he said. He had nicer luggage than I ever imagined him having. Marlena must have splurged before sending him away. Nice. "I got one more coming."

"Good deal," I said. "I'm so glad you came."

I tried to convince myself that this would be a good move for Blake. Verbalizing it, true or not, was the first stage to making it come true.

"I'm so happy to be here," Blake said. "I already wrote out a list of all the music producers and studios I need to get my demos to. And I got a list of the top modeling and music agents you can take me to. But that's once we do the touristy stuff... Santa Monica Pier, Disney, Universal, Roscoe's Chicken and Waffles, WeHo, Santa Monica Boulevard..."

"What do you know about WeHo and Santa Monica Boulevard?" I laughed. "Who you been talking to?"

"Facebook friends, duh," he said and smiled. I forgot. Nineteen-year-olds made online friends long before they met them in person. This was going to be fun. "Did you get me a car?"

"You think I'm rich or something?" I said.

"I thought everyone in California is rich," Blake said. He was serious. The media had pulled a fast one on the rest of the U.S. Just ask a homeless teenager in Hollywood or a disabled veteran on Skid Row in downtown L.A. or a family of six living in a two-bedroom in East L.A. The palm trees, bright lights, beach houses, and red carpets were for a very few privileged folk in L.A.

"Well, to answer your question about the car…nope. No car," I said. "But maybe you can borrow my Prius when I see how you drive."

"Awww, Unc."

"Awww, Unc nothing," I said and smiled. I could see his resemblance to Marlena's and my father, and that was kinda nice.

"I finally got my license," Blake said. "I'll take you on a test drive when we go clubbing one night. I heard about this place called Catch? Or Micky's? Or Circus? that's supposed to be hot on Tuesdays. We should go. And don't worry…I got an ID made before I left Indiana."

"Too much information, Blake," I said. "Let's just get your bags and get home. I made some turkey chops, corn, and applesauce. Your favorites."

"Yay," he said. "Because I ain't have any money to get any food on the plane. I'm starving. But I could stand to lose some fat and gain some muscle, for when I go on auditions."

Blake didn't have any weight to lose, being as skinny as he was, but I was more concerned with Marlena's frugality.

"Your mom sent you out here with no money?"

I was ready to get Marlena on the phone right away to ask how she intended for Blake to be taken care of this summer. Times were tight, but Marlena had seniority and an almost six-figure salary working overtime and split shifts at the auto plant, one of the last open and in production during the recession. She could have sent him with something. I guess she also thought I was rich because I lived in California.

"I bought this luggage at the airport before I checked in

for my flight," he said, like nothing. "Couldn't arrive in L.A. with Granny's old-school green Samsonite."

Priorities of a nineteen-year-old. I sighed. At least I wouldn't have to cuss my sister out. But I would have to talk money management with my nephew.

"You...are a mess," I said. "Where's the movie?"

"They left. They were following some girl from last year's *Big Brother*. She was on the plane, but only had her purse and little dog."

"You mean photographers and reporters?"

"I saw Stephanie Hernandez from *Paparazzi Players*," he said. "I tried to get in the background of the cameras. So we have to watch tonight and see if I'm in the shot."

If paparazzi were here for someone from *Big Brother*, that meant they might...

"Where's your other bag?" I asked. "We might need to get out of here pretty quickly."

"Why?"

"My friend who drove me to pick you up," I said and then got close to his ear to whisper, "is Tyrell Kincaid."

"The basketball player?" Blake asked, loud enough for the continent of Australia to hear.

"Shh, yes."

"No shit. You for real, Uncle Malcolm?" Blake said. He was beaming with excitement. "See, you *are* rich. I didn't know you roll like that. My uncle got famous friends. I'ma get my rap contract after all. I know he gotta know people."

I wanted to tell him that every young man comes to L.A. wanting to be a rapper or an actor (or any other dream job people come to California for), but the dream often doesn't come true. Instead I told him, "My friend has a busy life and a lot of other things to worry about."

"But since we'll be in the car with him," Blake pleaded. "Please?"

He grabbed his second bag off the conveyer. I took the one he'd already claimed. We rolled toward the door.

"Leave Tyrell alone, don't bother him," I said. "No demands or questions."

"Awww snap," Blake said. "Another movie shoot. Look."

I looked ahead and saw Tyrell's Lexus truck surrounded by paparazzi. The truck Blake and I were to be riding in. The scene was like nothing I'd seen before. Seemed like a billion lights, cameras, reporters were in the area. As Blake and I continued toward the truck, all lights, cameras, and reporters turned to us. The traffic cops cleared a little path for Blake and me to walk through, though the lights and action were blinding and difficult to navigate through.

"Are you the porno prostitute who brought down the house of Tommie and Tyrell?"

"Who taught you your moves and techniques?"

"What's next for you and the basketball player?"

"Any words for Tommie Jordan?"

"Were sex lessons part of your work with the LADS group you founded?"

"Was LADS an undercover porn shop?"

I thought, *I'm not the celebrity. Why are they after me?* I'd never been asked so many intrusive and embarrassing questions. Being asked in front of my nineteen-year-old nephew who had just arrived in L.A. was even worse. I mean, a prostitute? Was that what I'd been reduced to because of those damn videos Deacon uploaded to the Internet? Damn, the reporters were fast in connecting unrelated, but kind of related, dots.

"Make way for them," one officer shouted as the trunk of Tyrell's truck opened up. That same officer grabbed the bag I was rolling. Another grabbed Blake's, put them in the truck, and shut it. Yet another opened the front passenger and rear doors for Blake and me.

When the doors shut, Tyrell calmly said, "Let's roll."

He moved forward, inch by inch, as traffic cops tried to clear a path for Tyrell to drive through the cameras and reporters.

"Blake, this is Tyrell Kincaid. Tyrell, this is my nephew Blake."

"Good to meet you, Blake," Tyrell said and turned around briefly. "Sit back, man. We're about to take off full blast in a sec."

"Dang, Unc," Blake said and looked out each of the truck windows, which were surrounded with paparazzi. He was happily fascinated. He took out his own camera to film the paparazzi scene "That's dope. This is so freaking beat. Thanks for letting me come to California this summer."

"Put that camera away, Blake," I yelled. "And say hello to Tyrell."

"Whassup, Tyrell," Blake said.

"That's better," I said and gave Blake the you-better-shape-up eye.

"You look just like you do on TV and in the magazines," Blake said, as he stared in awe at Tyrell. So country.

"You follow sports?"

"A little bit," Blake said. "But mostly just to see who's cute. You know who's gay? Because I got a long, long list of players I'd like to do some thangs with."

Tyrell laughed and said, "Your nephew's funny, Malcolm."

"Wait 'til the peeps back in Indiana see this," he said proudly. "I'm famous now. And Tyrell Kincaid thinks I'm funny. I think this Hollywood thing is gonna work out."

After the officers cleared a path, Tyrell zoomed out toward

the airport exit and jumped on the 405 freeway. Definitely not the way to my apartment in Silver Lake. I didn't ask, and Tyrell didn't tell. At least, not yet.

Tyrell drove without saying much, but we listened to KJLH's Tammi Mac and Don Amiche afternoon show. Every hour, on the twenty mark, they did a roundup of Black celebrity gossip, which I was sure Tyrell wanted to hear. How this scandal played or died out in the Black community could determine a lot for Tyrell's and Tommie's standing in it.

Blake sat in the backseat, sending text messages, videotaping the drive on the giant freeways, as he called them, and enjoying his first adventurous night in L.A. To him, this was like being part of a movie—our initial paparazzi encounter and Tyrell outdriving the few reporters who tried chasing the truck.

I knew this was far from a movie and that real lives of real people were at stake. I had some explaining to do to Blake.

CHAPTER 19

The best way to describe where Tyrell took us first—it looked like it belonged in a music video. Specifically, it looked like it belonged in a music video for a rap or R&B star—clean, flat lines; minimal; lots of glass; lots of white; and set off with an infinity pool that flowed into the Pacific Ocean on the horizon. In fact, I was sure I'd seen the house in videos for either Ron Isley, in his Mr. Biggs phase, or 50 Cent back in the day. One of them. The house, it turned out, did belong to a rap/R&B star...and a basketball player.

"This is where I live," Tyrell said as he turned off the truck near the front door. We'd driven a good half mile from the automatic gate before we arrived to a circular driveway. "But that might be changing. I wanted to stop and get some things. Hope you don't mind."

"All right," I said. "We'll wait out here."

As fascinating as the whole hanging out with Tyrell had been, part of it seemed scary and weird. Like I wasn't worthy of being around him or in his world. Tyrell's house, his life in the public eye, his interest in friending me. It was just too much to take in.

"Well, I wanna go in," Blake said and opened up the back passenger side door. "I ain't come from Indiana to sit in a car all day."

"Blake," I said and gave him the eye again. "Chill."

"No, come in," Tyrell said and chuckled. "I might need a witness. In case we run into crazy."

"This is so dope," I overheard Blake whisper to himself. He had his video camera out again, taking video of the scene. I didn't blame him, but didn't let on. I was overwhelmed with the immenseness of it all. "This is a freaking dream."

"Are you serious?" I asked Tyrell. "Maybe we shouldn't."

"You should," Tyrell said and pointed to a two-seater Mercedes convertible sitting in the driveway. I couldn't name the model, but apparently it was safe enough in Tyrell's neighborhood for the owner to leave the keys on the hood. "Besides, that's his manager's car. Tommie won't get too crazy with Hamilton in the house."

"If you say so," I said. "I don't want to add to any drama between you and your man."

"The drama's already here, so you might as well meet him. You too, Blake," Tyrell said. "Give your friends in Indiana something to talk about."

We got out via our respective doors. Blake's camera was rolling, taking in the sunset behind the house, the roar of the ocean, the fancy cars parked outside, and Tyrell's height. I caught him taking a peek, a double take, as we walked to Tyrell's front door.

Once inside, we were greeted with a bottle of vodka crashing against one of the glass walls. It spashed everywhere but on us. I stayed quiet—so did Blake—and watched the scene play out in front of us.

"You bastard." I heard what I assumed was Tommie's voice. "You finally came home."

"Hello to you, too, Tommie," Tyrell said calmly, once we walked into the living room. "What's up, Hamilton?"

It *was* a music video living room. Minimal furniture,

clean lines, views of the infinity pool and ocean. I couldn't believe I was seeing Tommie Jordan up close. Seemingly crazy Tommie Jordan, who threw bottles of vodka across rooms. He was a hot brotha, with his dark skin and body for days. Looked just like his videos, but skinnier—the fifteen-pound camera rule. I'd actually listened to some of his music when he was in the teenybopper R&B group Renaissance Phoenix in the '80s and '90s, but hadn't followed his newest music, which was primarily singing hooks on rap and hip-hop songs.

"Well, you know the deal, Tyrell," Hamilton said. "Where's *your* cleanup team?"

"I'm not sweatin' this, I'm not the one in P.R. trouble," Tyrell said. "I'm just picking up a few things and I'm out."

"You can't leave me," Tommie said and charged toward Tyrell. "I need you. I need you."

"He does," Hamilton said, his eyes pleading for Tyrell to stay and listen. Even if only for a few minutes. "We were just starting our talk…about the situation."

"Tommie and I talked this morning, after he strolled in after the quakes," Tyrell said. "I know all I need to know. I'm out."

"Kick a Black man while he's down," Tommie said. "Fine. You do that."

Tyrell motioned to Blake and me. "I'll be just a few. Wait here or wait outdoors."

Tyrell left the living room and left Blake and me with Tommie and his manager. They continued their conversation as if we weren't there. In fact, it dawned on me they'd never asked who Blake and I were, nor did Tyrell introduce us. I guess since we weren't celebrity, we were invisible and didn't count to them. Shade. Still, I couldn't believe the details they spoke of in front of us. This was as good as *The Bold and the Beautiful*.

"He just don't understand, Hamilton," Tommie said and walked to the glass wall facing the ocean and sunset. If this were a movie, it would have been a perfectly framed shot for Tommie's next confessional lines. "It's not him. I love my Tyrell. I just love the rush, the chase, the idea of being with something new and exciting that requires no strings attached, no obligation, feeling, or emotion. My Tyrell knew that back when I had the fling with Rafael and then the others. It's just something new and different, but they don't have anything to do with how I feel about Tyrell. With him it's love. With the others it's…nothing."

Hamilton, Tommie's manager, looked good in his suit and unbuttoned dress shirt. He almost looked presidential. He was playing with his iPad while responding to Tommie.

"You need Jesus," Hamilton said, as emotionless as someone saying they needed to add soap to their grocery list.

"What?" Tommie asked, still staring out into the ocean and sunset.

"You got a response?"

"To what?" Tommie asked.

I kept my mouth shut. I hated the dumb act played by men who wanted to be victims and not take responsibility. Or pretended to not hear a question they didn't want to answer. I'd seen it with Deacon when he told me about his cheating and when he tried to deny releasing the videos of our sex life online. Now I could see why Tyrell was ready to get out. I sensed another topic for LADS—good men, bad dating choices.

Then I remembered I didn't work for LADS anymore.

"You need Jesus," Hamilton said again. Looked like Hamilton was growing impatient too. "You!"

"What Jesus got to do with me having my picture taken in a sex club? Or being escorted out by a rescue crew?"

"Hel-LO," Hamilton said and gave Tommie that eye a father gives to his young son. He put his iPad down on a glass-top table with an expensive-looking vase on it. "You said it, not me, Tommie."

"Still. I pay you twenty percent of all my deals," Tommie said. "You need to remember that without me, your income would drop significantly."

"Exactly!" Hamilton said.

"So what's the plan, Hamilton?" Tommie pleaded. "I'm not about to lose Tyrell, my career, this life I'm used to. I done made too many comebacks to make another one."

"Let's sit," Hamilton said and motioned for Tommie to join him on the sofa. "Now, I hate this because we're both gay and I don't believe in jumping in bed with the Black, religious ministrati, but those women who love you will buy it."

"I ain't gay, Hamilton. I'm open-minded."

"Whatever you want to call yourself these days is up to you," he said, and put on a pair of nice frames, just barely on the tip of his nose. "You need to join the biggest mega-church you can find, donate a ton of money to one of their causes—abstinence training, marriage and family counseling, something like that—and get some photo ops with some of the ministers campaigning for that so-called 'Family First' legislation in the upcoming election. I would say you had this in the works *before* these pics and vids went public."

"What? You serious?"

"I got the contacts at congregations in L.A., Atlanta, Chicago, Philadelphia, and Houston. Take your pick. They're all big. They're all Black. They all do the same thing. Kinda like you, hmm, Tommie?"

Hamilton grabbed a folder out of his man bag. Man done his research quick. Well, I was sure one of his assistants had done the research for him.

"This is crazy," Tommie said. "Not even the pisser has had to repent this much."

Hamilton slapped his hand on his knee.

"I'm trying to help you, Tommie," Hamilton said. "What's crazy, Tommie Jordan, is that you and Tyrell have everything, and so much to lose. And you go out and get your dick sucked by a man at some place with a bunch of strangers, and you get a bunch of damn pictures taken of you in the act while an earthquake is going on. That's crazy."

As much as Tommie hated it, Hamilton was speaking the gospel. I wanted to add an "amen" but didn't. This invisibility was nice, in a weird way.

"And so…?" Tommie said.

"Black gay R&B singers don't recover their careers like straight ones who fuck up."

"True."

"Especially when I have young, hot men on payroll to take care of the needs of my male celebrities who need a little trip to the other side," Hamilton said. "So you guys don't have to get caught in a bind like this."

"Yeah, I know."

Tommie looked like he was five and in trouble, especially when Hamilton pulled off his frames and stared at him.

"So we'll do a few photo ops with ministers, get you in *Jet*, *Ebony*, on Tom Joyner and Steve Harvey radio shows. Get you on Wendy Williams and in the Livonia Birmingham column before they come for you. Say it was research for a role, that you're doing the Black version of *Brokeback Mountain* or something. The women who love you will fall for it, you'll keep the masculine mystique going, and that's all."

"True."

"If you want, I'll call up Candace and see if she'll go to some of the upcoming awards with you," Hamilton said.

"I can't stand Candace," Tommie said and snarled his lips. "Let her play the nameless, silent, banging body, mixed-girl thing with someone else who into dudes."

"Which is why I keep her on call, and on payroll," Hamilton said. "For moments like this when they wonder if you're gay or not."

I'd heard about these young women like Candace, who walk the red carpet with male celebrities, appear to be in love with them in photos at parties, and kiss them at just the right moment during live red-carpet interviews. But I thought it was all just gossip made up by gay men who fantasized about male celebrities. Ruthless business, being a celebrity.

"Nah," Tommie said. "I'm not feeling the Candace charade now."

"Then how about doctored photos." Hamilton picked his iPad up from the table. He clicked a button, and some photos projected onto one of the white walls. "Everybody's got a computer these days. Anyone's head can be put anywhere. No pun intended."

I saw tons of pictures of Tommie in various pornographic shots and positions with women, men, three-ways, anything you can think of. Blake perked up, like a horny nineteen-year-old would, and I wanted to have him leave the room. Tommie looked horrified.

"I *know* I never posed for or took these pictures," Tommie said.

Now I got his point. Hamilton was good and cunning. Like a good manager was supposed to be. I wished I'd had a Hamilton helping me earlier in the week when I met with the LADS Board of Directors.

"We spin it with the whole Photoshop, crazed-fans thing," Hamilton said. "And no one will believe it's you in those sex club pics and vids. Or if they do, there will be enough reasonable doubt in their minds…and in the meantime, the church thing will be in full swing. Now, being seen with the rescue team after the earthquake and coming out of that place…that's your film character research."

"Cool."

"Pick your church of choice and I'll do the rest," Hamilton said. He stopped beaming the pictures on the wall. "Oh, and you're recording a duet with that one gospel singer…the guy who wins all the gospel music awards and says he's been 'cured' of his attraction to men. His people are excited to spread Jesus's word and reach out to the masses with Tommie Jordan singing hooks."

"I don't do hooks," Tommie said. "I sing lead."

"You want your career?" Hamilton said. "You're doing hooks for gospel."

"Gospel? Are you serious? I ain't sang gospel since belonging to the Hemmings' church back in Detroit."

I saw a light, an aha moment in Hamilton's eyes.

"I forgot the Hemmings family connections you have… Keith, right? Reverend Hemmings and the largest church in Detroit," he said. "I might have to work that angle in your salvation. You still talk to Keith or his family?"

"Um, well," Tommie said. "It's been a while."

"Don't answer, I'll handle that part," he says. "Call me in the morning when you're sober and clear-minded. We'll get Dr. Bentley here for STD testing. And no more crises, Tommie Jordan. And definitely no late-night creeping to sex clubs and sex parties. You hear me?"

None of this had anything to do with me, but it was interesting to see and hear. Part of it was sad, though, seeing how controlled and untrue Tommie's life was about to be. Even more sad was that Blake and I weren't even a blip on Tommie and Hamilton's radar.

Tyrell returned. Finally. He had a couple of garment bags folded over his left arm and a matching duffel bag in his right hand.

"So I see how it is, Tyrell," Tommie shouted across the room. "Step out on a brotha while he down and out. You leaving me for *that*?"

Tommie pointed at me, though he could have been pointing at my nephew Blake, since we were all in the same general direction. I was surprised to finally be acknowledged.

"No, Tommie," Tyrell said. "I'm leaving you for me."

CHAPTER 20

When we pulled into the alley behind my apartment building, I gave Blake my apartment number and key to let himself in.

It was almost eight in the evening, and after a cross-country flight and the post-flight drama at the airport and at Tyrell's and Tommie's, I knew Blake had to be hungry. But Tyrell didn't want to chance eating anywhere in public, since the Tommie/Tyrell story had hit the air, so I told Blake where he could find his favorite turkey chop dinner and to get started without me.

With Blake gone, Tyrell parked behind a car I didn't recognize, but knew was probably one of my neighbors or a visitor to a nearby apartment. He turned off the lights and the truck.

"Your nephew is cool," Tyrell said.

"Thanks."

"Like his uncle."

"I'm going to have my hands full this summer," I said. Wanted to change the subject quickly. "His mom—my sister—thinks I can help him get his life on track. He's nineteen and just wilding out on her lately."

"We'll get him on track," Tyrell said. "Once this whole

thing blows over, I'll get at you and we'll see what happens. I know you need some alone time with Blake."

"After what he experienced today," I said, "I'm sure he'll need therapy. Welcome to L.A., Blake! Now, let's go see your therapist and get you some mind drugs."

We laughed. On the radio, a Tommie Jordan song was starting to play. Tyrell changed it quickly to a jazz station.

"Loser," Tyrell said.

"Be nice."

He turned my way and stared. "You're so nice. I mean, the whole LADS work, community service thing. You're educated. Together. Look good."

I wanted the compliments to stop. So I rebutted wtih, "Older than you. Unemployed. Not famous. Definitely not an athletic body. Poor…compared to you."

"It's not a money thing," he said. "I'd give it all up to be happy and have peace of mind like you seem to have."

I smiled. "'Seem' is the operative word."

"Still," he said, still staring at me. I was feeling a little uncomfortable with the attention. "I'm not saying this because I'm some famous baller who knows he can get whomever he wants—because I can…"

"Whatever, Tyrell." We laughed again.

"But I think you're smart enough to know I dig you," he said.

"Me? Why?"

"Yeah, you."

"Are you serious?"

"Yes."

"Wow," I said. "I'm shocked."

"Why do you think I took that hundred-dollar speaking gig at LADS? I researched *you*, Malcolm."

He grabbed my hand with his dinner-plate-sized hands.

I couldn't wait to tell Kyle about the fingers. The places my mind went. I was getting a bit…excited.

"It was three hundred," I said and laughed.

"I woulda done it for free just to get to meet you," Tyrell said. "For real for real."

"Oh God," I said. Blushed. "I don't know what to say, Tyrell."

"Don't say yes or no," he said. "I'ma get a room at The Standard or Mondrian, lay low for a few days, maybe a week. Settle this Tommie thing. Then see what's up. You do wanna see what's up, don't you?"

"What's up? Like…" I pointed to Tyrell and me and back to Tyrell with my free hand. "Us?"

"I know you thought about it."

"No," I said and grinned. "Really, I haven't."

"I have," he said and lowered his voice. "Anyway, I wanna get to know you, Malcolm Campbell."

If we'd been dating, or had known each other for a lot longer, this would have been the kiss moment. But it wasn't, and it left a lot to look forward to. A lot.

"Cool," I said, like a nerd who doesn't have a clue. "I'm glad I could be of some help or support."

"I've got good intuition," he started to say, and when I flipped the radio back to Tommie Jordan singing, he laughed and said, "Okay, maybe not. You got me."

"Oh really?"

"Yep," he said and moved in for the kiss that seemed destined to happen when…

A flash from one photographer's camera lit up the evening sky, and the car parked in front of us sped off.

"Fucking reporters," Tyrell yelled and blew his horn.

"Outside my dinky apartment? My God," I said. I was surprised too. If this was how life with a celebrity could be, friendship or relationship-wise, I wasn't sure if I was up for the challenge.

"Outside your dinky apartment," Tyrell said. "I should chase his ass down. Motherfucker. Sorry for cussing, man. That's not me. Damn Tommie."

"It's deserved."

He reached over and grabbed my hands again.

"That means there's more where that came from," Tyrell said. "I hope you can deal with being in the spotlight a little."

"I'm not a celebrity, this is *your* life," I said. My defenses were up, realizing that my video situation, which I thought was dying down, was now linked to Tommie Jordan and Tyrell Kincaid. "I'm just someone trying to help young Black queer guys."

"Which is why I like you so much," Tyrell said and squeezed my hand. "So when I get back at you again, you let me know if you think you can handle it."

Big responsibility for something I never wanted or imagined happening. Life in the spotlight.

CHAPTER 21

Blake was lying on my living room couch, a plate of half-eaten food on the nearby coffee table, watching the footage he'd recorded on his camera.

"Damn, Unc, we got the whole thing on camera," Blake said as he continued his camera viewing. "If I was a little digga nigga, I could sell this to *Paparazzi Players* or *TMZ* for big bucks. Lord knows I could use the money."

"But you're not going to sell it, nor will you upload the footage online or onto my computer," I said and scooted Blake's legs aside so I could join him on the sofa. "Nor will you use the n-word in my house."

"Oh my God, you and Ma are the same about that word," he said. "And yes, I know that word is beneath us. Heard it all my life from Ma, Grandma, everybody."

At least some of the Campbell family good home training stuck. I was sure most of it had, underneath the rough edges.

"Yep, we don't use it," I said. "Anyway, Tyrell is my friend, and if we want it to stay that way, that camera is staying here and locked up forever."

"Of course," he said and smiled. "I'm not shady pines like that."

"Good to hear. You're not as bad as Marlena said you are."

"Oh God, Ma," he said and leaned up. He grabbed my

arm and pulled me in for a hug. Grown as he and his mom thought he was, Blake was still only nineteen, still a teenage boy. "Thanks, Uncle Malcolm, for letting me stay with you this summer. If I had to live in that house one more day with Ma, I don't know…"

"No problem," I said and hugged my nephew back. "I wouldn't have it any other way. Of course, there will be rules to follow."

"Awww, Unc. I'm an adult." He made a face that let me know he wasn't quite there—an adult—yet.

"You're staying in my house," I said. "There are rules. But we'll talk about those in the morning, after you've settled in and all. It's been an exciting few hours in L.A. for you, huh?"

"So what's up with you and Tyrell Kincaid, Unc? He is so…damn, if you wasn't up on that…" Blake said and made a little sound with his mouth, like he was sucking in air. "And you know Tommie Jordan too? No one back in Indianapolis knew you was rolling like that with the famous people."

"I wish," I said. "There's a lot to explain. But first, I'm hungry. Did you eat up all the food I cooked?"

"Nah, Unc," he said. "But you could forgo a meal, it looks like. That don't look like a six-pack under that shirt."

"I'm thirty-five, Blake. I've earned that paunch," I said and we laughed. "Let me grab a plate and we'll talk."

I got up from the sofa and walked to the kitchen. On my way, I looked at myself from the side in one of the mirrors I passed. It wasn't that big. But it wasn't Tyrell Kincaid or Tommie Jordan tight either. They were paid to have six-packs. I wasn't. But with my new unemployed status, I could be a permanent gym rat. It would give Blake and me something to do, working out and bonding over gym boy crushes.

After fixing my plate—with less food than I would

normally eat, since Blake had me all self-conscious about my little paunch—I joined Blake in the living room again.

"When can I meet some of the guys at your work, Uncle Malcolm?" Blake asked. "I want to meet some guys my age, not just your friends. Though your friends are cool because they're famous. They're just…old…for me, ya dig?"

At some point, I knew I'd have to explain to Blake, and even to my sister Marlena, why I wasn't working a daily nine-to-five anymore. I'd wanted to talk to Marlena first, just to give her a heads up and prepare her, though she'd probably get some indirect scoop about me from Tommie and Tyrell's scandals on the entertainment shows tonight. That was if I wasn't too invisible to be considered a newsworthy sidebar to Tommie and Tyrell's drama.

"So, Blake, there's reasons why your mom is strict on you," I said. "They're the same reasons I'll be as strict on you. Because I don't want you become a statistic, or go through the same dramas and heartaches I went through growing up. It's why I started LADS and wanted to work with the young guys. Too much out there for you to get into."

"Is this the message moment?" Blake grinned. When I didn't grin back, he said, "Oops, just kidding. Go on."

"So I met this guy a couple years back…" I started.

For the next hour or so, I explained to Blake about Deacon, our breakup, the sex videos posted online, meeting Tyrell, the LADS Board of Directors, losing LADS, the earthquake, and Tommie/Tyrell. Blake had questions, which I answered honestly, so that he understood why my life was complicated at the moment. In between questions and answers, Blake and I snacked on our lukewarm turkey chops and applesauce.

"So other than that, Mrs. Lincoln, how was the show?" Blake replied.

"Huh?"

"Just playing, Unc," he said. "Well, I think you're handling all this very well. A lot more calm and controlled than I probably would be."

"Well, I did toss Deacon's laptop in the pool," I said and smiled. "Highly inappropriate thing to do. I don't recommend it. I mean, in the long run we're all brothers and we need to support and uplift each other. That's why I started LADS."

"But what about when your so-called brothers don't support and uplift you?"

"You think about the bigger picture," I said, not quite convinced I believed what I was telling Blake. But I knew flying off the deep end was not the way to teach a young man like Blake how to handle life's challenges.

It was then I realized how much I would miss the work with LADS, and helping young men like DeMarco and company become the men they were meant to be.

"You're so deep, Malcolm," Blake said. "I'm really glad to be here with you this summer."

"I'm glad you're here too," I said. "In the morning, we'll talk about the rules for staying here. Because you're not having the revolving door of Hotel Blake like you did at your mom's house."

"Huh?" Blake asked. "What you talking about?"

"My sister says you were the human mattress of Indiana," I said. "That's *not* going to be the case in my house."

CHAPTER 22

I thought after the high drama of the day before, Blake and I would have a low-key day around the apartment.

There was still some cleaning of his space to do, and Blake needed to unpack and make his room feel like his own. But that could wait for a while. Blake was still sleeping, and snoring up a storm. With the time change from Midwest to West, I was surprised he wasn't awake with the morning sunrise.

After calling Marlena and updating her with *my* version of the past few days' events, I made a short to-do list for the morning. Mainly things I could do within walking distance of my place. That was one of the reasons I liked living in Silver Lake. Everything you needed was within a few-block radius of where you lived—markets, street fairs, restaurants, and bars. A mixture of old and new buildings, apartments and houses, Silver Lake housed a diverse mix of young professionals, immigrants, hipsters who thrived on blue-collar living even with their million-dollar trust funds, and artist/creative types. I had lucked out years earlier finding a rent-controlled apartment with a landlord who knew all the residents and their families by first name.

I set a bag of trash on the landing outside my apartment, knowing I would take it to the building's garbage bin in the alley when I came back from my errands. My plan was to walk over to a fruit market, florist, and newsstand on Hyperion early in the morning. I wanted to pick up some bananas and lemons, an assorted bunch of flowers just because, and the *Los Angeles Times* before it got too busy with people starting out their morning routines.

The morning air was crisp, clean, and cool. Not a hint of smog anywhere. Perfect running weather for the jogger taking a stretch across the street from my building. I knew the weather would soon give way to the dry heat that went with L.A. summer days. As I walked toward Hyperion, I noticed that the one single jogger I'd seen just outside my apartment grew to six. They were running alongside me as I walked my morning errands. They all had cameras and questions. The scene grew from nothing to something in a matter of minutes.

"How's the video career?"

"So is the ball player good in the sack?"

"When's the wedding?"

"How many three-ways have you done with the baller and the singer?"

"How much are they paying you for your services?"

"How many positions can the basketball player play off the court?"

I had no media training. But I knew to pull my hoodie over my head and turn around to walk the one block back to my apartment. I called 9-1-1 like numerous other celebrity-lites did when they found their paths blocked by paparazzi.

"Nine-one-one. Where is the emergency?"

"I'm in Silver Lake. Near Hyperion and Sunset Boulevard."

"What's your emergency sir?"

"I'm a regular, everyday citizen, and I can't even get through the pathway to my apartment," I said as I continued walking. I almost tripped over a photographer who'd gotten on the ground trying to shoot an up-angle picture of me.

"Can you be more specific how this is an emergency sir?"

"The paparazzi and cameras are out of control. They came out of nowhere and are following me everywhere."

I imagined the operator taking down my story in preparation of dispatching the police. Instead, I got, "Excuse me, sir, but who are you again?"

CHAPTER 23

Finally I made it back to my apartment building. About fifteen minutes later, and without any assistance from the police. Thanks, but no thanks. My everyday status didn't raise a blip on the emergency radar of LAPD.

The trash bag I'd left before the morning attempt to run errands had been opened and the contents strewn across the landing at my front door. Reporters. They were good and hungry for any dirt they could get on me. And I wasn't even the main attraction. Tyrell and Tommie probably got a thousand times more paparazzi scrutiny. But they also had a thousand times more resources to keep the reporters and photographers at bay. They also had fans who would support them. I had nobody who'd advocate for me.

I decided to phone Kyle for advice as I sat down at the kitchen table with a hot green tea and the *Los Angeles Times*.

"Well, well, well, Mr. Snag A Baller," Kyle said as he picked up his work phone. "I saw some picture of you and Tyrell going in for, or pulling away from, a kiss. Must be nice."

"We didn't kiss," I said. "Where you see this at?"

"Girl, let me email you some links." He laughed. "Of course, they're focused more on Tommie and Tyrell, since they're the moneymakers. But all the Black and gay gossip sites gave the story top billing. I'm surprised your phone isn't ringing off the hook, or no one's banging on your door trying to snap a picture or interview you."

"No, they're after me too," I said. "I tried walking a few blocks this morning to the newsstand and fruit market, and the photographers were all over me. Like six of them."

"Oh my God, Malcolm, are you serious?" Kyle said. "You need anything?"

"Like what? Privacy?"

"That's a start," Kyle said. "I can get you a bodyguard type like yesterday if you want."

"That's crazy," I said. "I just want to be left alone so I can give Blake a normal summer. We probably will need some groceries delivered, especially if I can't leave the house without all the…"

"Consider it done, my friend," he said. "Anything else?"

"Maybe you can stop by here today when you have time," I said. "This whole thing is crazy. Why would they come after me? Tommie Jordan's the one involved in a scandal, not me. He's the one that got this whole thing initiated."

"Malcolm, let me school you on how Hollywood works," Kyle said. "The legitimate news sources won't give any time to the story. Black gay men don't make real news. They don't even make tabloid news. Sad, but true. But the gossip sites and the bloggers…girl, some of them will be and are calling you the home-wrecking porn star because of those videos your ex put out there. Some are saying you, Tommie, and Tyrell did threesomes on a regular basis. But whatever. No one really knows the truth but Tommie and Tyrell, and I know you're no home-wrecking porn star. The good part is that tomorrow, there will be more gossip about other people and this will all be forgotten."

"And archived on the Internet forever," I said. I sipped my green tea. "This is so embarrassing. I'm not a home-wrecker, and I'm far from a porn star. I don't even know Tyrell that well, and I didn't really know he and Tommie were together until Tyrell took Blake and me to their house."

"You went to their house?"

"Yeah."

We were silent for a few seconds.

"I was right about him liking you, huh?" Kyle asked. "Girl, you got a baller sprung on you."

"Who likes me is the least of my worries," I said. "It's weird, but yeah. I think he likes me. Don't ask me why."

"I know Malcolm Campbell isn't fishing for compliments," Kyle said. "Of course we all know you're smart, fun to be around, good-looking...and has Tyrell seen those videos of you yet? Because I'm sure he'll be happy to know you got skills in the bedroom too."

I smiled at Kyle's attempt to make me feel good about what I'd have to offer to Tyrell.

"As far as I know, he hasn't seen the videos...yet," I said. "We haven't talked about the subject. But he's gotta know by now, with all that's coming out about Tommie and their relationship and my so-called little connection to them."

"We'll get you an agent and write a bestseller when this is all over," Kyle said. "I have to get to a meeting, but I'll swing by later to see you and meet your nephew."

"Cool," I said.

"Hey, you should turn on *The Black Morning Radio Show*," Kyle said before hanging up. "My assistant just handed me a note. Tommie Jordan's about to do an exclusive interview. Supposedly his version of what went down."

CHAPTER 24

Tommie was good. Or at least his agent Hamilton was, in prepping Tommie to sound convincingly full of it.

"I am a family man and a man of God," Tommie said to the male host and female sidekicks of *The Black Morning Radio Show*. "I'm raising a young niece, who is an orphan, and who fortunately is away at boarding school in Vermont. I just thank God she has not been subjected to the rampant lies and innuendo about my personal life and career."

I rarely listened to *The Black Morning Radio Show*, preferring the live and local broadcasters on L.A.'s independent stations in the morning. I liked the comedic aspects of *The Black Morning Radio Show* sometimes. The journalistic standards were often pushed aside so that Black entertainers could push their products shamelessly or spout the lines their publicists came up for them. The host and team of *The Black Morning Radio Show* were giving Tommie an open mic. Basically.

"So let's just set the record straight," the host said. "Because I've been the subject of rumors in my personal life, and I know what this game is all about. This is your platform to tell us *your* side before they tell *their* side."

"Thanks, man," Tommie said. "I knew I could count on you and my community to listen. We know it's all a game, but the average listener doesn't know how this works. First of all, my agent got me in a movie—a legitimate movie—about the lives of sex addicts. It's a small art-house film that will probably get a lot of attention at awards season, and I'm playing the role of a bodyguard and assistant who has to help his gay client keep his sexual addiction out of the public eye. To get in character, and to understand the lives of people who will do anything for sex, including having dangerous encounters at sex and swinger clubs, I started doing a little research—because I don't know anything about that lifestyle."

"Right, right," the host said. "I've been in movies too. You want to be as authentic as possible. It's not just reading some words on a cue card. It's about being in character."

"So I was recording some tracks in the studio one night," Tommie continued, "and I noticed these guys—only guys—going in and out of this discreet little building across the street from the recording studio. I asked around, got the information I needed, and knew it'd be a good place to take a break from recording and do some research for the film."

"Right, right," the host encouraged.

"And you know I'm well-known," Tommie said. "I'm not gonna announce I'm Tommie Jordan while I'm in one of these establishments observing what's going on. But there are a lot of haters out there, especially if you're Black and trying to make it in the public eye, you know about that…"

"We all know about haters," one of the female sidekicks chimed in and giggled. "*The Black Morning Radio Show* gets hated on all the time."

The whole interview was starting to make me sick. Like puke sick.

"Oh, and did you know the person who tipped off the paparazzi got fired from one of the tabloids, but got forty thousand dollars for that footage? They won't tell you that part."

"Forty thousand? Get me that gig for a day's work," another female sidekick chimed in.

"White reporter?" the host asked. It didn't matter, really, but I knew what the host was trying to get the audience to sympathize with.

"You know it," Tommie said. "My team did some investigating and found all this out. They are always looking to keep a Black man down. You see how the Republicans are treating Obama, and he's barely been in office six months or so."

"Amen," the host said. "Now, what about these rumors about you and the basketball player, Tyrell Kincaid?"

"I'm glad you brought that up," Tommie said. "Let me assure you and the audience of *The Black Morning Radio Show* that Tommie Jordan is absolutely, under no circumstances, not gay. I've known Tyrell Kincaid for almost five, six years when we met at a charity basketball tournament in Los Angeles. I think you played at that one too, don't you remember?"

"I sure do," the host said. "It was just a bunch of us old and young folks out there raising money for needy children and literacy programs in L.A."

"And at that time in my life and career, I was a little down on my luck. But I was still there for the children. Tyrell is a good man and offered me and my orphan niece use of his oceanfront house until I got my career back on track. He's hardly there, with the basketball season, ya dig? Tyrell Kincaid is kind of like my landlord."

I wanted to shout out to the radio that Tommie Jordan was a liar who used the same tired homophobic arguments to keep not only himself down, but also many of his fans who could have been gay or lesbian as well. That kind of simplistic argument, utilized to bait people into staying quiet about gay issues in the Black community, was why places like LADS were still important.

"Everybody could use free rent these days," one of the female sidekicks added. "Times are hard for everyone in this recession."

"Amen to that," Tommie said. "So can I talk about my new campaign and cause?"

"Go ahead, brotha," the host said. "This is where we get to tell our side to the people who matter."

"Thanks," Tommie said. "I just recorded a dope gospel track with a young cat over in Atlanta. Hip-hop beats, word of God, all that."

"Anything to get God's word out there," the host said. "Why gospel at this point in your career?"

"I felt it was time for my career to serve others," Tommie said. "This song's going to be the theme for the Family First initiative in the upcoming election season, where we want to ensure that our kids know that the best families are those where one man and one woman are heading it up. Traditional families, like we grew up in, ya dig? All the proceeds are going to the campaign, which is being headed up by a fine man in Los Angeles, a man of God named Reverend Lamont Murphy, who runs this organization in L.A. called LADS. It's about the upliftment and empowerment of young Black men who find themselves confused and at a crossroads in their lives about who they are."

My jaw dropped. Tommie and Reverend Murphy were teaming up to support the Family First initiative, a dangerous attempt to modify the state constitution and legally define marriage. And they were using my organization—my former organization—LADS, to do it, and announced it live on *The*

Black Morning Radio Show. The show was national, airing in hundreds of markets, with millions of Black listeners across the country. Tommie and Hamilton were super strategic. And connected. Unlike most people with image management issues in their lives.

I'd learned how to work with and challenge the city establishment when I founded and ran LADS. But learning how to work with and challenge the Black entertainment establishment was another story, especially when a male-dominated, heterosexist, performing masculinities narrative kept the same images and stories recycling over and over about Black life in the U.S.

All I could say out loud as I slammed my cup of tea on the table was "Oh hell naw."

CHAPTER 25

"Dang, Uncle Malcolm," Blake said as he walked into the kitchen with his laptop computer in his hands. He was more animated and excited than I'd expected, considering how hard he was snoring just an hour earlier. "I can see why those paparazzi people are all up in your ass. One of my friends just sent me a link of you on GayClick. I had to break out the tissue and shut the door."

The conversation was gross, and highly inappropriate for an uncle and nephew to be having. And after listening to the lies Tommie Jordan spewed on *The Black Morning Radio Show*, I was on edge and not in the mood for Blake's happy-go-lucky and no-thinking attitude. I instructed Blake to have a seat and to shut down the computer.

"First of all, I'm an adult and you need to address me as such," I said. "Regardless of how much you think you know me or how cool you think I am, I'm still your uncle. And you're just nineteen. Don't forget that!"

"I didn't think I was..."

"You said it right...'I didn't think,'" I said. "You always have to think, Blake. You always have to consider other people and be considerate. So that means you don't step to an adult like one of your boys. I'm your uncle, and we're on friendly terms, but I'm not your friend like that."

"Sorry," he said. "I just thought since we're roommates this summer, and we're both gay, and you're the coolest uncle in the world that we could just talk like that. I mean, after all we went through together since I got to L.A. Sorry."

"I guess I can see how you'd get confused," I said. "But you're my nephew living here. Not a roommate. You don't pay rent. And your mom would appreciate it if I looked after you like she would."

"Oh God," Blake said and sighed. "Here we go again with rules."

"They're simple rules," I said. Because he was family, and with a legal obligation to his future, I knew I had to be Campbell-family strict and lay down the law. "No guests in this house unless I know who they are. No going out with people unless I know who they are. No drugs in my house at all, and I'd prefer you not use outside my house either. I'd make you keep your laptop out here in the living room or kitchen, but I'll give you some leeway on that. No late-night anonymous sex chats or visitors here."

"Come on, Unc, that's how my generation meets people. Your generation too, truth be told," he sighed. "You and Ma have been talking, huh?"

I knew he knew Marlena and I had been talking about him. He was usually nearby whenever she would call and complain about Blake's revolving door of sex partners, smoking out, or not studying. It was Blake's track record, not my need to be a control freak, that warranted a set of house rules. Marlena had sent my nephew to stay with me, and she sent him with certain expectations in mind.

"And stop playing dumb, Blake," I said. "You're nineteen. You need to be focused on what you want in life…something more than who you want to sleep with or who you meet online.

And you need to be back in someone's college or community college. I mean, what do you want to be in life?"

Which may or may not have been a fair question. When I was nineteen I was focused on being a sophomore at Northwestern University, but didn't know how that would translate into a specific job or career. And for someone like Blake, who'd been in and out of trouble in school and barely earned his high school diploma, developing a focus might have been too much to ask. I hated being a pragmatist about Blake's potential, but someone needed to focus him so he wouldn't waste his time or future.

"You know I want to be a rapper...or a model...or someone who puts together outfits for celebrities..."

I wanted to roll my eyes and tell him what I saw as reality. Those jobs were statistically not a reality, and a lot of it— potentially working in the industry—was based on lies. Not the way we were raised in Indiana. That I'd seen and heard numerous young men from LADS talk about their dreams of celebrity, but the realities of life left those dreams deferred. That often the young men who wanted those types of jobs didn't have a clue where to begin to map the path to their goal.

But I didn't want to be a dream killer to my nephew, at least not yet, and decided to engage him. I needed to develop some rapport in order for him to accept my feedback.

"So what is your plan? Or let me rephrase...what have you learned about how one becomes a rapper, model, or stylist?"

Blake was silent as he thought about my question. "What do you mean?"

"Okay," I said and took out a piece of paper. I felt like I was at LADS again and doing a one-on-one with a client. "Let's do stylist. Put 'stylist' at the top of the page. Put yourself today at the bottom, with your current skills, training, networks, and qualifications. Make a list of all the baby steps and the time frame you think need to take place for you to achieve that goal at the top of the page."

"I don't know all that," he said and smiled. "That's why I moved to L.A. and that's why I have an uncle with famous friends. Y'all will hook a brotha up."

This time I did roll my eyes. I huffed too. My patience was wearing thin. I wondered how Blake could have been surrounded by all those hardworking Campbell family members, and none of that drive for middle-class status and values reached his core. It was sad, but similar to what I saw in some of the guys at LADS. The system had created barriers related to race, class, gender, and sexual orientation that many individuals knew, or experienced, could kill their personal dreams and aspirations. Even in the age of Obama. Still, I had to have hope Blake wouldn't give up. We didn't give up—the Campbells.

"It's about hard work, not hook-ups," I said. "Life is not that easy. Especially if you're Black, without an education, and gay. Please. You're *nobody* to larger, mainstream society, that's why you have to have a goal and some knowledge and a degree behind you. Work harder than anyone else."

"Ma says the same thing all the time," he said. "I'm beginning to think I don't wanna be an adult if it's all doom and gloom."

I thought about what Blake said. Somewhere between nineteen and thirty-five, life transitioned from fun and spontaneous to something a little less than fun and spontaneous. That was just the reality of life, though present situation notwithstanding, I'd had more good days than bad.

"I guess we have a lot to learn from each other this summer," I said. "But for the record, I never consented to those videos being made. And they were all with the same person, who I was in a relationship with. That's why you have to watch who you get involved with, because not everyone who seems nice is. But that's another story for another day, Blake."

I patted his leg to let him know we'd be all right. The way my dad would reassure me after one of his life-lessons lectures.

"See, Unc, that's all you had to say and I would have been cool," he said. "You have a lot to learn about young people this summer."

"And you have a lot to learn about your uncle," I said. "Now, since you're so wanting to get into entertainment, get online and pull up *The Black Morning Radio Show*."

"Why?"

"I want you to listen to today's show and think about what we saw at Tommie and Tyrell's the other day," I said. "And then tell me five reasons you think going into entertainment is going to help your community."

CHAPTER 26

K yle kept his word.

Within an hour of our phone call, I had a personal safety assistant outside my apartment and two others watching the front and back entrances of my building. It felt weird—having people—but being drawn into the scandalous world of Tyrell and Tommie made it necessary. I prayed the situation would die down and go away in a few days.

By noon, Kyle showed up at my place with what seemed like a trunk load of groceries, which the security team helped to bring in. He also brought lunch—Thai food—for Blake and me. I welcomed the company. Blake, after I introduced him and Kyle to each other, welcomed the food. Thai was something new to his Indiana-bred taste buds.

Kyle and I sat at the kitchen table. He put a napkin, bib-style, over his white polo shirt and covered his khaki pants. I missed being part of the working world and longed for the day when I could get back into a nine-to-five. Kyle dived into his pad thai and into the conversation.

"Wasn't that some bullshit?" Kyle said. "I can't believe they let Tommie Jordan go on and on without even asking one intelligent or challenging question. But then again, I *can* believe it. How are you doing?"

I was somewhere in between. I was happy my best

friend was with me and supportive. I was livid with Tommie Jordan and the interview on *The Black Morning Radio Show*. I hated that Reverend Lamont Murphy was using LADS as a platform to support the hateful and discriminatory Family First Amendment.

But I loved the Thai food Kyle brought.

"Kyle, I'm all over the place," I said, finally. "If I wasn't a stronger person, I could see how one might end up overusing alcohol or pills. That's not cute."

"Don't even go there, my friend," Kyle said. "I see too many folks around the studios who think the answer is in a bottle or prescription…or worse. Functioning zombies."

"Don't worry, I'm not going there," I said. "I just want a sense of stability back in my life like it was a week ago. Imagine me, Mr. Boring Does Everything Right, being an Internet porn site star, fired from my job, and embroiled in the unfolding drama of two closeted Black celebrities? If they could see me now."

"Girl, they probably have."

We laughed.

"That was a little bit funny, Kyle."

"Might as well laugh," Kyle said. "People overcome scandal every day. Little by little you'll get better and get back to that sense of stability you want. Hell, stability is boring sometimes."

"What? Mr. Been In A Relationship Forever?"

"As much as I love Bernard, sometimes I want to try something or someone new," Kyle said. "Then he comes home with a funny story, and his good-ass cooking, and I realize we make it new every day. Then I get over my thoughts."

It was the first time I'd heard Kyle verbalize any questioning about his relationship with Bernard. It was kind of a big deal to me, because they always presented a united and happy front. But we were best friends. We talked about random subjects all the time without making them big deals. Just getting stuff out there with no real conclusions or advice.

"Thoughts?" I asked.

"We're human," he said. "But when I think of what's out there—or *not*—I put those thoughts away. I've never cheated, if that's what you're thinking."

"None of my business if you have or haven't, Kyle," I said.

"I've had offers," he said. "But there's no one like Bernard, and I'm not starting over at thirty-five. Couldn't imagine it."

"Okay," I said. "Because I'm not throwing any breakup parties."

"Of course not," he said and smiled. "I'm throwing your bachelor party when you marry Tyrell Kincaid. He wants you, you know that?"

"Whatever."

"I have a feeling," Kyle said. "I think when all this blows over, you and Tyrell will be making some of your own videos."

"Stop."

"Those long, big hands and fingers."

"Stop."

"Hot, sweaty basketball player all up in your stuff."

"Kyle."

"Here," Kyle said and reached for Blake's video camera he'd left on the kitchen table earlier. "Let's record your thoughts...or let me...how does this damn thing work? We'll start our own channel online. Wouldn't that be funny?"

"Don't ask me, I'm not that tech savvy," I said. "It's Blake's."

Kyle and I heard sound coming from the camera after he'd pushed a couple buttons.

"...*abstinence training, marriage and family counseling,*

something like that—and get some photo ops with some of the ministers campaigning for that so-called 'Family First' legislation in the winter election. I would say you had this in the works before these pics and vids went public."

I looked at Kyle and said, "That was Tommie's agent, Hamilton."

We continued listening to the sound coming from the camera.

"What? You serious?"

"Is that Tommie?" Kyle asked.

"Yeah."

"I got the contacts at congregations in L.A., Atlanta, Chicago, Philadelphia, and Houston. Take your pick. They're all big. They're all Black. They all do the same thing. Kinda like you, hmm, Tommie?"

"We should get Blake in here," I said. "He can get the picture to come on. BLAKE...GET IN HERE. Look at us, a couple of old, college-educated guys can't figure out this camera."

"This is crazy. Not even the pisser has had to repent this much."

"What's crazy, Tommie Jordan, is that you and Tyrell have everything, and so much to lose. And you go out and get your dick sucked by a man at some place with a bunch of strangers, and you get a bunch of damn pictures taken of you in the act while an earthquake is going on. That's crazy."

Blake walked into the kitchen, not moved at all by the sense of urgency with which I'd called him. I got a sense of why Marlena was always yelling at him—to get him to *do something.*

"Whassup, Unc?"

"How do you get pictures to show on this?"

I pointed to his video camera sitting on the table.

"Dang, Unc," he said and picked it up. "I got some private videos on this."

He pushed one button and sat it back on the table. There wasn't any video, nor any more sound coming from the camera.

"We don't want to see your little nineteen-year-old thing on camera," Kyle said.

"You shouldn't even be making those kinds of videos," I said.

"I bet." Blake grinned. "I know how y'all dirty old men like the young bucks."

"Blake. Serious," I said. "Turn on the camera."

"Why?"

"Because I said so," I said. Put a hand on my waist and tilted my head like I meant business.

My nephew was three seconds away from a backhand across the face in my mind. Of course, I knew I'd never do it. Violence was never an answer. However, I could empathize with my sister having dealt with Blake solo for nineteen years. And with him looking so much like his father, who'd abandoned Marlena and Blake shortly after his birth, I could see how Marlena could have so much anger when Blake acted like this. A backhand was a bit much, though, when my frustration was with people other than Blake. I decided to take another approach.

"Blake," I said. "You're interested in a career in entertainment, right?"

"That's whassup," Blake said. "Why?"

Kyle was intuitive and knew where I was going.

"You might be one step closer to getting the career you want," Kyle said. "Turn on the camera for your uncle and me, and you'll see just how close you are."

CHAPTER 27

It took some coaxing, but eventually Blake bought into our plan and showed us what he'd gotten on camera. We—Kyle, Blake, and I—decided that laying low for a week would help, and thanks to Kyle's huge grocery purchase and the security person posted outside my apartment, it was possible to lay low successfully.

Throughout the week, Blake updated me on what the bloggers were saying and not saying about Tyrell and Tommie and me. I read a few, but lost interest in the untruths being passed off as truths. As time passed, my name disappeared altogether and the stories focused just on Tyrell and Tommie. A few days later, their scandal was no longer the top read or blogged-about gossip in the Black or LGBT communities. The message boards were drying up, with no new and false comments about me and my role in their relationship. The syndicated radio shows were through with their constant Tyrell and Tommie gossip and speculation, as newer and more scandalous celebrity incidents were taking place center stage.

All the while, my phone was not ringing with calls from Tyrell.

The lack of contact from Tyrell was fine with me. It wasn't like he and I were long-lost friends, nor were we anywhere close to a romantic relationship. I chalked it all up to vulnerability, celebrity insecurity, a nasty cheating incident involving public sex, and frustration with being forced into silence about his reality that led Tyrell to lean in for that kiss that almost happened. It was all fine, I told myself, though Tyrell being on my mind meant something else. I just had to block Tyrell from my thoughts, I told myself.

Now it was time to put everything in motion that Kyle, Blake and I had talked about.

The thought of going back to LADS was humiliating in itself, though it was necessary to what we hoped to accomplish. I'd never been fired from a job. And since it was a high-profile position, and working with young people, I didn't know what impression the young people at LADS would have of me. I imagined that Reverend Murphy and company had to have done a hatchet job on me and my reputation after I left and they took over.

But now that the gossip sites were done with me, I could start moving forward.

My fears were eased a bit when DeMarco's face lit up as I walked through the door with Blake.

"Oh my God, Malcolm," he said and ran around the desk to me. He planted his arms around me and squeezed like he'd missed me his whole life. I'd never seen DeMarco dressed so conservatively in our time working together. Reverend Lamont Murphy must have implemented a dress code.

"DeMarco, you look great," I said. "And so professional."

"Ha, very funny. This is the new boring workplace uniform," DeMarco said and modeled his blue polo shirt and khaki slacks. "I never thought I'd see you again. Are you coming back? The guys, we all miss you here."

"No, not at all," I said and saw the disappointment in DeMarco's face. "I'm here to pick up some of my leftover things and take some of my files off the computer."

"Take me with you, Malcolm," he exclaimed, and then whispered, "I hate it here. It's like church…but *mean* church. Who's this?"

DeMarco eyed my nephew up and down, in more of a "he's cute" way than suspicion. That probably meant Compton was no longer in the picture or that the gloss of their new relationship was wearing dull. Funny how quickly those relationship things die at that age.

"This is Blake," I said. "My nephew from Indiana. He's staying with me for the summer."

"That's whassup," DeMarco said and bumped his fist against Blake's. "I heard about you. You should add me on whatever sites you use."

Blake smiled and said, "Fo sho."

"I hope your uncle Malcolm has been showing you the sights…what young people like to do, not his generation," DeMarco said. "Or maybe not, knowing how serious Malcolm can be?"

"I'm a prisoner at his place…all the damn paparazzi," Blake said. "This is our first time out in about a week. Thank God."

A young people reunion, talking about their "old" uncle and former boss, was not what I returned to LADS for. As nice as it was seeing DeMarco again, I didn't want to get attached to what I was missing at the organization.

"Is Lamont Murphy here?" I asked. "I need to get into the office and computer, if possible."

"He's at a Family First campaign luncheon in Long Beach," DeMarco said. "He should be gone for a couple hours, I guess."

"Good," I said. "Do you mind if Blake goes with me? Technology…I'm old, don't get the stuff."

"Yeah, but I need to log you in," DeMarco said. "He

changed all the damn passwords to Biblical names, and he monitors all our computer use from his office. Troll."

"Are you serious?" I asked. Of course, what supervisor wouldn't change passwords in the office when following someone else's leadership?

"Yep," DeMarco said, a bit of sarcasm in his voice. "Real dope, huh? Real muthafuckin' dope."

"Well, you were the king of Facebook and whatever else you used to look at when I worked here."

"And all the Audre Lorde, James Baldwin, Octavia Butler, and Bayard Rustin quotes on the walls...gone," DeMarco said. "All the books you used to keep in the library by E. Lynn Harris, James Earl Hardy, Keith Boykin, Daniel Black, Rashid Darden...gone."

As DeMarco, Blake, and I walked down a long hallway to my former office at the back of the building, I noticed all the quotes I'd had framed and along the walls were gone and replaced with Bible verses. Not that I minded the Bible, or spirituality, for that matter; I just thought a little balance and open-mindedness was important too.

"Wow," I said. "I didn't think you paid attention to my work."

"I did...we all did," DeMarco said. "We just didn't want you to know we were paying attention."

"Geez, thanks, DeMarco."

"No worries," he said as we entered Lamont Murphy's office, my former office. "Just don't want you to think you made a difference, Malcolm."

"Yeah," Blake added. "Don't let it get to his head."

DeMarco sat at the desk and logged in for me.

"It's all yours," DeMarco said. "I need to get back to the front desk, so let me know when you're done so that I can get his computer back to how it was."

"Fo sho," Blake said. "I'll help him...old people and technology, ya know?"

DeMarco and Blake shared a quick laugh before DeMarco went back to the LADS reception desk. Blake took out what he needed and connected to Lamont's computer.

In a way, I felt bad for lying to DeMarco. The day I'd been fired I transferred all my work and personal projects to an external hard drive. I wasn't too tech deficient not to figure out that part.

But adding information to a computer was a whole 'nother subject, and thanks to my nephew Blake, I was well on my way to completing that goal.

CHAPTER 28

That evening, after Blake and I finished our business at LADS, I decided to invite DeMarco and some of the other guys from the group over to my place for dinner. On my way out the door, DeMarco had handed me a certified mail package. It turned out to be my buyout from LADS, almost six figures—thank God taxes were taken out—which was enough for me to live on for at least a year in L.A.—two anywhere else—though I didn't want to be without a job for that long.

Having the guys over was part victory party, since Blake and I had completed the first part of our plan for justice. The other part was recruiting the young men to participate in the next step of our plan.

And what victory and looking-to-the-future party would be complete without a feast of good-luck foods? Bernard, Kyle's partner, had my apartment smelling like a New Orleans restaurant with all the foods many of our families mythologized as luck-producing. Seafood gumbo with thick chunks of crab, okra, shrimp, and tomatoes stewing on one eye of the stove. A pot of black-eyed peas simmering on another. Fluffy white rice sat on the side, ready to be scooped up and garnished. For those over twenty-one, there were authentic Hurricanes, mixed up by Kyle, who loved a good drink as much as I did. For those under twenty-one, there was red Kool-Aid to at least give the semblance of enjoying an adult good time. Next time Bernard had an audition for the Food Network, I'd be sure to organize a letter-writing campaign pleading for him to have his own cooking show.

Blake was in a good mood, finally getting to be around young men his age in L.A. We'd crammed close to twenty LADS in my living and dining rooms. He turned up his iPod mix featuring the latest in hip-hop and rap that they all could sway their heads to, while keeping their heads down and focused on their personal music, tablets, and phones. Definitely a party for the twenty-first century, but for today it was all fine. I needed my army of LADS men to start a campaign for change.

"I'd like to propose a toast," I said and banged a spoon against my glass. I opted for red Kool-Aid, just to make sure I was levelheaded. "To you...all my fine young men from LADS. Without you, my work would have been nothing. I wish nothing but the best for you in this time of transition at LADS, and during this time of blatant dislike and disrespect for young men like you with Lamont Murphy and the Family First initiative. Stay strong and know that you'll always have support from me."

Most cheered and clinked glasses with each other. DeMarco shared a sloppy kiss with Compton, apparently still his man o' the day, whose presence made me a little uncomfortable and Blake a little jealous. Anyone could see that Blake and DeMarco had a little attraction toward each other, but I decided to stay out of it for the moment. I decided against telling DeMarco that his man had been trying to get at me weeks earlier at The Abbey. No need for mentor/mentee drama.

"Well, I want to say something," DeMarco chimed in. "We all know why you got fired, Malcolm. And it's okay. We've all seen your videos, or watched porn online, and some of us—

I'm not naming names—have posted ourselves up doing the do. No shade. We don't judge you at all. It makes you like one of us, and we love you and will do whatever it takes to get you back at LADS or running another program for guys like us."

"Okay." A few guys clinked their glasses as they spoke out in agreement with each other.

I had to interject a little so the young men wouldn't think I was aspiring for a career in Internet porn.

"Now, I wouldn't willingly put myself online like that," I said. "My ex made those videos without my knowledge while we were in a relationship, and he posted them without my permission. I wasn't out having random sex with random people."

"That's cool," Compton said. "They still dope."

"That's my uncle you talking about," Blake said, shooting a dirty look across the room to Compton. "Watch yourself."

"He's the one talking about being sexually empowered," Compton shot back at Blake. "I think it's not wrong to record yourself and make a little cash on the side. I'm sure you wouldn't know about that, Blakey."

"Guys," I said. Wasn't looking to referee between a stranger and my nephew. "Regardless, I took responsibility and faced my punishment. Fair or not. But there's something bigger at stake."

"Like the lies out there about my uncle and Tommie Jordan and Tyrell the ball player," Blake said. "Did you hear how Tommie Jordan disrespected you all and LADS on *The Black Morning Radio Show* the other day? How he lied about my uncle's work and his own sex videos?"

The room got silent as Blake got on his own nineteen-year-old soapbox. I was proud to see him step up.

"I know it's all lies," Blake said. "Trust me, my uncle and I have proof."

"But how can it be lies if Tommie Jordan said it on the radio?" Compton said. He hadn't been part of LADS, so he wouldn't have known what many of the other guys had learned about questioning everything. "That's against the law."

Kyle emerged from the kitchen with Bernard and jumped into the conversation.

"I'm Kyle, Malcolm's best friend," he said as he joined Blake and me at the center of the room. "I work in entertainment. I'm an attorney and agent. One thing I can tell you about the world of entertainment—none of it is real. It's all made up. People lie every day to get a deal, get you to buy something, or to get ahead in the industry."

"Okay, Mr. Big Shot, and what?" Compton said defiantly. "What's that got to do with old boy here dropping it like a porn star?"

"Who asked *you* here?" Blake shot back to Compton, and stepped closer as if to challenge him.

"Yo, Uncle, who wanted to give me some of that good good," Compton said and walked toward the front door. "Fuck y'all. I'm out. You coming, DeMarco?"

If I'd been in DeMarco's head, I could have imagined the conversation going on—good dick or good friends?—as if there were really a choice. Figured I might have to explain to DeMarco about The Abbey, Compton, and me after all.

In the midst of the argument and commotion, Bernard ducked his head in the living room doorway with his chef's hat and apron on.

"While we're waiting for the next exciting episode of *Hot Gay Mess*, why don't the rest of you decide if you're going to come on in here and eat, or watch the drama?"

The guys erupted in a mixture of laughs, amens, and heads turning from Bernard to Compton to Blake. Most, however, headed toward the kitchen while Compton walked out of the apartment—without DeMarco. I was glad that Bernard broke up the tension with the main reason I brought the guys from LADS together—food.

As the young men returned with their plates piled with Bernard's culinary delights, Blake and I started making our plea to enlist their support.

DeMarco, armed with a new confidence since standing up to Compton just minutes earlier, said, "No need for a presentation. Whatever you want from us, Malcolm, you've got."

CHAPTER 29

MalcolmDeservesHisJob.blog.com

I don't know if you know my former boss, Malcolm Martin Campbell, but if you did, you'd know he was a good man and that all the lies that the singer Tommie Jordan is spreading are just not true.

Posted by Anonymous

WeHateTommieJordan.blog.com

How can someone who's part of us do so much against us? That's exactly what Tommie Jordan, the supposed singer now of gospel music, is doing to the Black, gay community. He's turning his back on those who supported him all his career. You know what I say? I say we turn our back on his career and stop crushing on him, stop buying his music, and stop going to his shows. Hell, better yet, let's all go to his shows, get front row seats, and let him (and all those straight women without gaydar) know who puts the butter on his toast…who puts the lube on his you-know-what!

Posted by Anonymous

ShadyTJ.blog.com

I don't know about you, but I'm so glad we have a place like LADS where Black, gay men learn to support each other and not pull all that shade that society expects of us. Especially when it comes to so-called celebrities like T. Jordy, who's trying to have a hip-hop career with his old ass. I digress with disrespect. If any of you listened to his whack-ass interview on *The Black Morning Radio Show*, you heard nothing but shade and disrespect being thrown at a community that T. Jordy is a part of. Hell, everyone has seen him on Sundays at The Abbey, of course trying to pass himself off as a "straight ally." "Straight ally" my ass. If anything, he tried to get all up in my ass one sunny Sunday at The Abbey, but he wouldn't want y'all to know about that.

Posted by Anonymous

The Livonia Birmingham Show

They say there's nothing worse than a Black woman scorned, but I'm telling y'all that the wrath of the Black gays...ain't no joke. Michael, roll this footage from last night's Tommie Jordan performance at the Morning Star Mega Church in Atlanta. The boys were all up in the house of the Lord, supposedly to watch Tommie Jordan premiere his new hit gospel duet. The performance was your standard ToJo show. But just as he got to his climax of the song, the black gays, who had mixed in with the church first ladies, all stood up and staged a kiss-in...in the house of the Lord!!! Lawwwwd, watch the clip as Tommie and the church all went quiet during the non-violent love protest. Talk about a premature release... all Tommie Jordan could do was walk off and the show was over. So much for Family First! Thanks, boys, for the tip... and the clip...If you got vids you want to share, get at your girl Livonia Birmingham!

CHAPTER 30

I couldn't tell if the LADS guys were making an impact or not, but maybe I was expecting too much to happen too soon.

Within a few days of the dinner party Blake, Kyle, Bernard, and I had thrown, three new blogs from the guys sprang up online. And a couple of LADS had created their own channels on YouTube and uploaded their own video blogs about the scandal. The content wasn't as objective as we'd suggested it to be and came across as more of why-Malcolm-Campbell-was-done-wrong propaganda. Not that I expected work the quality of Morrison, Baldwin, or McMillan to come from the guys. For most, this was their first serious writing since high school, and for those who'd completed public school in L.A., that wasn't saying much.

Still, I was proud of their work. And soon, their work and activism caught the eye of more popular Black, gay news sites—Rod 2.0, Clay Cane, Keith Boykin, and Jasmyne Cannick—to drive traffic and interest to their work. *The Livonia Birmingham Show* clip was a coup and brought national attention to gays in the Black community.

But for every good clip that brought attention to the larger issue, there were those sites—both the gossip ones and the conservative ones backed by Family First supporters—who brought attention to me…and the videos posted online of me by Deacon. I knew I'd never escape that part of my life. But neither could Tommie Jordan, as more and more young, Black men came forth with their allegations of being hit on, or sleeping with, the new prince of the gospel music world.

Even with the mixed response to the online activism, I knew in the long run we would prevail and get LADS back, defeat all who supported Family First, and earn my reputation back as a hard worker who cared for causes larger than myself. Getting my name back would have been enough. But the young men really loved LADS and hated seeing how it had changed since Lamont Murphy's appointment as executive director.

I needed to curtail my frustration and stay focused. Keep my eyes on the prize, as the old folks would say.

Chapter 31

Two weeks later, with our story being out of the news, life was getting back to normal. Blake was out and about in L.A. with DeMarco and some of the guys from LADS. I thought it would be a good time to call my sister to give her an update on her son's visit to L.A.

"What's going on, little brother?" Marlena said. She sounded excited when she picked up the phone. "How's my boy?"

"Blake is fine," I said. "He's hanging out with some of his new friends. He's a good kid. People like him. He's got a good head on his shoulders."

"You sure it's not an act? That boy is quite an actor."

"So far, so good," I said. "We've been getting along just fine."

"Well, he don't call noboby," Marlena said. "Is he there? Can I speak to him?"

"He's out right now," I said. "He's got some friends and they're showing him the so-called cool sites of L.A. I think they're over at Universal CityWalk now, then Roscoe's later."

"That's good," she said. "I knew sending him to L.A. for the summer was the right thing to do."

"Well, considering the circumstances he dropped in on…I guess so."

"Your little video-ho thing," Marlena said and chuckled. "Blake told me about the little boycott thing you wanted to start against Tommie Jordan. Me and all my girlfriends love us some Tommie Jordan. No way I was gonna be able to participate in that. Sorry, Malcolm."

"I see. Thanks for the support."

"Thank God Mama and her church friends don't get into all that celebrity gossip stuff online or on TV," she said. "So you don't have to bring this up to her. She's out of the loop."

"Good to know." I was happy knowing I didn't have to explain everything to my mom. It would be too much for an older woman raised in the Midwest all her life, and who prided herself on raising the perfect son.

"Y'all and that fast living out in L.A.," Marlena said. "But you'll be happy to know I turned down two grand to talk to Livonia Birmingham about you. She's good. One of her producers tracked me down at the auto plant."

"Are you serious?" I asked.

"As a heart attack," Marlena said. "I coulda used that two grand, but I wasn't about to sell my kid brother out like that."

"What did Livonia Birmingham want? About me?"

"I guess she wanted to get some dirt on you and Tyrell Kincaid," she said. "Of course I had nothing to give her but dead air and a dial tone."

I thought people were through trying to connect me with Black Hollywood's closeted super couple. I guess not.

"I appreciate you not selling me out, Marlena," I said. "But there's not much to say. I just gave him a shoulder to cry on after Tommie Jordan did his thing at that sex-club establishment and got caught. Everyone blew the rest out of proportion."

"Alleged sex-club incident," Marlena said. "I still don't believe Tommie Jordan is gay."

"Believe what you want," I said.

"And I can't believe you got a sex tape out there floating on the Internet," Marlena said. "Thank God Mama and her friends ain't into all that celebrity gossip. *The Young and The Restless* and *General Hospital* are enough for them."

"Thank God."

"Lord have mercy," Marlena said. I could almost envision her fanning herself. "These celebrities should be ashamed for pulling you into their mess."

"I'm not in it. I just want LADS back, and my name. I'm not looking for fame or money from this."

"That's what I wanted to hear," Marlena said. "I knew all this was a bunch of bull. Though you need to go kick that Deacon's ass for leaking all your kinky videos online. Blake will do it in a heartbeat, he's a fighter in case you didn't know."

I knew my nephew had a bit of a fighter spirit. But violence against Deacon wasn't what I had in mind. I'd already killed his laptop. That was enough for me.

"I know, Marlena," I said. "I'm trying to keep him centered and from doing anything stupid."

"Well, I love you, little brother," Marlena said. "And believe me, all those guys—Deacon, Tommie, Reverend Lamont, all of them will get their due."

"Thanks."

"And maybe you'll hook yourself a rich ball player in the process," she added. "Lord knows we could use a break."

"I think Tyrell Kincaid's a good boy in all this," I said. "I'm not even thinking about him."

My doorbell rang. Wasn't expecting anyone to visit me. Blake had his own key, Kyle was away for a conference in Vegas, Tyrell was off in seclusion, and paparazzi had died down but still had to stay a certain number of yards from my place. I peeked out the peephole. Looked like a driver, concierge type person. I hoped it wasn't a photographer type disguised to get more dirt on people I could care less about.

"Hold on, Marlena."

I opened the door.

"Your presence is requested at The Standard in an hour," the driver/concierge said and handed me an envelope. "He told me to tell you this is no trick and no paparazzi. He just wants you to join him for a dinner meeting at The Standard."

"Marlena, I'ma have to call you back," I said.

"Sounds like you've got a date?" Marlena asked. "So just call me later and we'll catch up. And tell Blake to call his mom sometimes."

"All right, I will," I said. "Thanks for listening."

"Anytime, little brother," she said. "Bye."

After we hung up, I told the driver/concierge I'd be just a moment. I looked at myself in the mirror. I'd put off getting a fresh lineup one day longer than I wanted, and I felt a little rough around the edges going to see Tyrell. On the night the paparazzi had snapped a picture of us in his truck, with Tyrell going in for a kiss, he'd mentioned getting a room at The Standard or Mondrian. Maybe he was ready to come out of seclusion and pick up where we left off. I just wished he'd given me a call or a little notice that he was ready to see me.

I smiled. Felt good to know that Tyrell still wanted to see me. Though he was still embroiled in his drama with Tommie Jordan, I knew this was his sign that my patience was paying off and that he was a man of his word. And if that was the case, Tyrell wouldn't mind an overdue haircut on me.

Chapter 32

It's funny how living in L.A., we all had our patterns. For me, my routine generally went Silver Lake to South L.A. and back to Silver Lake.

So as the driver/concierge wove through West Hollywood on Sunset Boulevard, I looked in awe at all the sites and people I normally didn't see on my daily routine. It was nearing seven thirty on a warm summer evening, and the streets were lined with people heading to chic restaurants for dinner. Every now and then I saw a paparazzi group swarming outside a boutique or storefront looking for the celeb-o'-the-day. Lucky me, my time had passed and I was out of the spotlight as something or someone juicier came along.

I called Blake as we pulled into the front of The Standard. He hadn't known I'd be out for the evening, and I thought it was the responsible thing to do—let him know where I was and that I'd be away, possibly all night. Blake didn't answer, so I left a voicemail to that effect for him.

The driver/concierge opened my door, which led to the sliding glass doors of the hotel.

"Your key is in the envelope I gave you," he said. "You're in Penthouse 3A. No need to check in at the front desk."

"Thanks," I said and reached for my wallet to give him a tip.

"No need," he said and swatted my hand away. "But you've been requested to leave your cell phone, so as to avoid any interruptions for your evening."

How romantic…Tyrell wanted a completely romantic evening, just the two of us.

"Thanks, but I can't," I said. I knew I could explain to Tyrell once I got upstairs. After all, I had Blake to watch after and couldn't just be out on a random Saturday without giving him any guidance. Tyrell would understand. "I'll let him know why."

The driver/concierge nodded, as if he didn't want to put up a fight. "Have it your way, Mr. Campbell," he said before heading to the driver's side of the car. "A car will pick you up when you're ready to go back to your…apartment."

"Thanks," I said and entered the sliding doors.

I had only seen photos of The Standard online and on those entertainment shows that featured fancy celebrity pool parties. I'd heard that it was the hangout spot for out-of-town performers, their entourages, and fans. The interior of the hotel looked a hundred times more impressive in its modern, sleek, and simple presentation in person than in pictures. I took the first available elevator to the penthouse level, anticipating seeing Tyrell for the first time in weeks.

The elevator exited directly into the penthouse. I saw an impressive dining table topped with lit candles, two plates of food topped with silver covers, and all the linens and flatware one would have for a romantic dinner for two. Patti LaBelle crooned in the background, but Tyrell was nowhere to be found.

"Hello," I said out loud. "I'm here, Tyrell. I got your invitation."

"You weren't invited…I sent for you."

Hamilton, Tommie Jordan's agent, emerged from a side room and walked toward me. He wore a satiny brown smoking jacket, similar to what one would imagine that old guy from Playboy or Penthouse wearing, and matching brown lounging pants.

He held out his hand. "I'm Hamilton James."

"This must be some sort of mistake," I said. "Tyrell Kincaid…"

"Hmm, you thought Tyrell Kincaid invited *you* here? For a romantic *tryst*? You're funny and not too bright, Marcus Campbell."

"The name is Malcolm, not Marcus," I said.

"I don't care about the name." Hamilton motioned for me to sit on the adjacent sectional in the nearby living room area. He sat across from me and poured two glasses of champagne. "To me you're nobody."

The whole scene reeked of shadiness, with a strong hint of Alexis Carrington Colby from the '90s.

"If I'm nobody, then why am I here, Hamilton?"

He handed me a glass and took a sip of his drink. No way would I share a drink with the Black devil of the entertainment industry. All the advice he'd given Tommie about the sex-club scandal worked for Tommie and backfired on me.

"You're here because you're—excuse for lack of class when I say this—fucking with my money," Hamilton said. His voice deepened and lost its professional edge and the hint of a British accent that he'd used the last time I encountered him— at Tommie and Tyrell's mansion. "I'm not about to have some 'hood-rat fags from South Central and two country bumpkins from Indiana fucking up my business or Tommie Jordan's career."

To my knowledge, the Internet blogging had gotten some

bites from national media, but I hadn't imagined it having any long-term effect on Tommie's career. Maybe I was wrong. Except for Kyle, I was out of the loop on the entertainment industry.

"Hamilton, do my speaking voice and good grammar sound like your average everyday 'hood rat or country bumpkin?"

"We're in L.A.," Hamilton said and swatted a hand in the air like he was getting rid of a fly. Of course, he was just being dramatic. The faux accent returned. "Everyone's an actor. Half of Black L.A. is fronting proper English."

"Well, I hate actors and everything about your phony industry," I said. "And I'm not particularly feeling being with you right now."

He held up his glass to toast. I declined.

"So you're probably wondering why you're here?" Hamilton asked. "I am too, but you're a lot tougher than I thought."

"Thanks for the compliment," I said. I held up my glass for a toast, but still did not drink from the devil's cup.

"You're nobody, Malcolm," he said. "Nobody. But I realize that it takes more than a fresh pair of Nikes to get you and those 'hood rats from LADS to learn their place."

I was confused. I couldn't have been a threat to Tommie, or Tyrell for that matter. I was doing my best to stay out of the public eye after the initial Tommie sex-club scandal and the insinuations of me being the third wheel in their friendship/relationship. Our plan to reclaim my name and get LADS back was not working, to my knowledge.

"Why am I here, Hamilton?"

"Look, I know you and Tyrell want to be together," Hamilton said. "And I think it's inevitable that it will happen.

They've broken up, but they're not divorced."

"Divorced?"

"They married in Massachusetts a couple years ago," he explained. "Dumb move on Tyrell's part since he makes more money and has the most to lose in a breakup, but he's a sentimental sap…like you."

"But what does that have to do with me?"

"Look, Malcolm, you can have Tyrell in time," Hamilton said. "But not while I'm representing Tommie. I'm doing my best to keep this 'gay' shit out the public eye so that Tommie can make a living for a little while longer, Tyrell can quietly get his divorce, and then both can be free to do whatever they want without losing their basketball or singing careers."

Hamilton poured himself another glass of champagne. I'd sat mine down on the side table. Still didn't want to break bread with the devil, but was enjoying Hamilton's antics as he got more and more buzzed off the champagne.

"So, Malcolm, if you can ride this out for just a few more months, you can have more money than you ever imagined because Tyrell can stay closeted and still play ball, and I can let Tommie loose to be a free agent—who listens to forty-year-old hook singers anyway—and I'm still in business."

Hamilton, if he was being honest, was offering me an alliance. My silence, get the guys from LADS to back off for a while, and I'd get to be with Tyrell. No strings attached. No drama. It all sounded good in theory, but there were too many variables I didn't know about.

First, I wasn't in this for Tyrell Kincaid. And I definitely wasn't in this for his money. I just wanted my career and to help my community. And what if Tyrell didn't even feel for me anything beyond a friend or confidant? He'd certainly been missing in action for weeks. What if anyone else—a judge, a courthouse clerk, someone who worked for Hamilton—leaked details about Tyrell and Tommie to the media? With all the tabloid news sources out there, anyone could make a few thousand dollars by sharing a document or opening their mouth. In this 2009 economy, anything was possible.

"I don't trust you, Hamilton James," I said. "Why should I believe you?"

"You don't have to," he said and sipped from his glass. "All you have is my word. And as you can see, my thoughts and my words make things happen. Tommie's got a career, still. And you don't."

Point taken.

"And what if I don't go along with you?"

"I know your nephew wants to be a rap star," Hamilton said. "But like most Hollywood wannabe types, he's been willing to do a little bit of work on the side. Like uncle, like nephew."

Hamilton pulled a remote control from his smoking jacket and turned on the flat screen monitor on the opposite wall of us. I saw my nephew Blake on the receiving end of Compton's and my ex Deacon's pornographic rage. In the background, a voice that sounded familiar was giving commands and directions for Compton's and Deacon's next moves on my nephew. How and when did Blake have time to go out of my house to make such a video? I was upset and saddened at the same time.

"Gay porn does not a rapper make," Hamilton said and smiled. "That's just raw footage. Wait 'til it's cleaned up."

"No way," I said. I was dumbfounded. Didn't know what else to say. Did a quick mental Rolodex of memories thinking of when and how Blake had time to hook up with Compton and Deacon and make gay porn.

"And there's more where that came from," Hamilton said. "My partners are really anxious to make some money off this one...a fresh face, a young piece of Midwest ass. Unlike the middle-aged uncle."

Hamilton turned off the sound. At least I wouldn't have to hear my nephew seemingly enjoying himself. Still, that voice giving directions...

"Why my nephew? I said. "This is between you and me. Leave Blake out of it."

"Looks to me like he's in it, on it, receiving it," Hamilton said. "Is this what you call Midwestern values? Hmm, maybe that's what we can call this one. *Midwestern Family Values.* Or maybe *Family First.*"

"You can't release that video with my nephew in it," I said. There was no way I would allow Hamilton to put that video out for the public. Nor would I allow Marlena to know what her son had gotten himself into since moving to L.A. "I can take whatever you dish out, but you're not going to mess up my nephew's life."

"Good. Now we're negotiating." Hamilton nodded. "I see you're the man of integrity they all say you are."

"I don't want that video going public," I said. "Turn it off. I don't want to see anymore."

Hamilton showed a little humanity and turned off the video. He walked to the dining room. I followed.

"Do we have a deal, then?" Hamilton asked.

"Yes, Hamilton, we have a deal."

At that point, I didn't care about anything but my nephew's future and reputation. Pursuing Tyrell was the last thing on my mind. That paternal instinct to protect those younger than me kicked in.

"Call off the LADS boys, the boycotts, the blogs, and

all of that other foolishness, and Tyrell will be yours on a silver platter—all his millions, no drama," Hamilton said. "Understood?"

"Understood," I said. I *was* done. I walked toward the elevator. Pushed the button. "I hope Tommie appreciates how ruthless you are. You're a perfect agent and manager."

"Thanks." He grinned. "Want to join me for dinner?"

"Not a chance."

"Have it your way," he said. "I'll have the car waiting for you downstairs…ciao for now."

The elevator arrived in time, before I could say something that might render the deal mute. I was this close to turning around and clocking Hamilton, but he held all the cards. I stepped in and rode down to the ground floor. Felt like I'd made a deal with the devil.

But knew it was better than letting my nephew's future hang out to dry.

CHAPTER 33

I t wasn't the way I imagined I would die.

Not that I believed I had a right to script the exact moment and manner of my last moment on earth. Somehow, though, I imagined that I wouldn't know when it was happening. Thought I'd go to bed after a grand evening with friends or family, and just not wake up. That those memories of a last festive evening would forever be sketched in the minds of the significant people around me. Or I thought I would wake up one morning and, as I was going for the morning paper, collapse just outside my front door. That I wouldn't know what hit me. That I would be old and have lived out my natural life, the way it should be…ideally. That my life would have felt complete and natural to be ending. A purposeful life that fulfilled its purpose.

Not the kind of death that would create headlines and questions.

"Mr. Campbell." I heard the driver's voice through the partition speaker. "I think we're having car problems. I'm going to pull over and check things out. You're free to step out while I figure out what's up."

Though it was nighttime by now, I was familiar with where we'd pulled over—somewhere in East Hollywood, where I could have easily walked or cabbed to Silver Lake. No need to wait for Hamilton's employee to drive me home.

"I can get home from…"

"Faggot." I heard a voice beside me as I walked to the raised hood of the car, where the driver was.

The man standing beside me was not alone.

"Fucking faggot."

Neither was the voice behind me alone. The same voice giving directions in my nephew's video. Lamont Murphy's voice.

Before it made any sense to me, before I could really comprehend what was happening, I felt the strike against the back of my rib cage. Felt the wind knock out of me. Felt myself lurch forward. The kind of blow I'd never received.

It came again, this time striking just to the right of where I'd been hit a few seconds earlier. Heard the smashing of glass. Getting me in a spot where it was impossible not to feel it, where it was impossible not to hear the cracking of bones, where even if I didn't want to react and fall, I had no choice but to. Had no control. Left side of my face against the asphalt. Cold. Rough. Hot. Felt my skin rip as I hit the ground. My face. Always the area I protected when I perceived myself in danger. Now I couldn't protect it…or myself.

Yelled. Thought I was. More like a whisper. A gasp of air. Sunset Boulevard. East Hollywood. Busy night. People should have been around. Someone should have been running to my rescue.

"Shut up, faggot."

Saw construction boots gain momentum, pull back, and accelerate toward my chest, then stomach, then groin. The force rolled me a couple feet along the ground. Gravel and glass sticking to my arms and face, like glitter on that

Styrofoam ball planet my dad helped me make in third grade. Floating. Kind of awake. Dreaming? Reminiscing?

Now facing the late-night sky. Saw the bat flying toward my face. Slow motion, yet real time. Little time to react. Felt part of the force on my elbow, part on the top of my head.

Why? Me? Now?

"That'll learn you, faggot."

Heard construction boots walking, then running. Two doors slam. Engine rev up. Tires skid as they drove away.

Afraid to move. Paralyzed in fear. Too tired to do anything. Looked at the night sky. Knew, well, hoped it would be minutes before anyone would find me. Wondered why merely being a faggot was enough to beat me, leave me. Felt tears forming in my eyes. Not the way I wanted to die, but ready.

Dreamed. Rested. Gave in to the pain. Relaxed. Prepared to let it be over.

CHAPTER 34

B lake said I had been unconscious for a day. After another two days of continued improvement and observations, Kyle drove Blake and me home. I'd escaped, they said, with mostly bruises and braised skin on my face. I guess I was physically tougher than I thought.

"You're lucky you woke up when you did," Blake said as we drove out of the Kaiser Permanente parking lot. "For a minute, I thought it was touch and go. I thought I was going to have to fly my mom or grandma out here, but I didn't want them to know what's going on."

The last thing I, or Blake, needed was for my sister Marlena to be in L.A.

"We're all trying to figure out why you'd be walking alone in East Hollywood at night," Kyle said. "That's not even your scene. The police thought it was strange."

"Especially since your car is still parked at your place," Blake said. "I mean, they were trying to call you all kinds of a crackhead prostitute, Unc, but I had to clear it up that you don't do any kind of drugs or illegal stuff. Still, they can't figure out why you have no memory of being out on the streets at night."

"It's just going to be one of those unsolved crimes until

you remember something," Kyle said. "But it's a hairflip now. You're well. You're with us. And now you're going home."

"Yep," I said. "I guess it's all a mystery."

I wanted to change the subject. Talking about my encounter with gay bashers wasn't on the top of my list at the moment.

"Kyle, you have any Nancy Wilson in your car?" I asked. "I feel like listening to that one song where she advises the poor woman her relationship is over."

"I know what you're talking about," Kyle said. With a press of a button, we were listening to Nancy Wilson's "Face It Girl, It's Over." And Kyle pretended that he wasn't that tech-savvy, though I knew he had over five thousand songs stored in his Cadillac's dashboard hard drive. "Love this song. Miss Wilson's telling the truth…face it, girl."

"I don't like this old music," Blake said and started putting his headphones on. Brat. "Y'all didn't believe in dope beats back in your day."

"This is before Kyle's and my day," I said. "But it's still good music."

"Just listen," Kyle said. "You might learn a thing or two about life."

"I know everything I need to know about life," Blake said and laughed.

If only Blake knew one thing. That I remembered everything, from the limousine ride to The Standard, to my meeting with Hamilton James, to being a captive audience to Blake's porno video in Hamilton's hotel suite, to getting beat up on the dark streets of East Hollywood, to hearing Lamont Murphy's voice giving directions in the video and just as I was attacked. I remembered it all, but chose to protect Blake's reputation by pretending not to recall what had happened.

We continued north until we hit my street. I was happy to see familiar territory. Silver Lake. The ride would give me a few more minutes to decide how and when to tell Blake or Marlena (or both) what they knew to be true, but I'd been naïve enough to wish was not.

That Blake would never change his ways.

CHAPTER 35

"Aaah, it feels so good to be home," I said when Blake and Kyle opened the door of my apartment and led me inside to familiar territory.

I really meant it. I felt like a free man. Not only was I free from the confines of my hospital bed, and the tubes and bland food, but I was free of the video drama of the past weeks, free of my job, free of Tyrell and Tommie, free of any men who didn't have my best interest at heart. It was nice to not have tabloids and photographers pursuing me for a story. Pretending like I didn't remember anything gave me a chance for freedom from all drama around me.

Then I looked at my nephew across the room, as he grabbed his laptop from the dining room table and took it into his room.

"What's that look for, Malcolm?" Kyle asked as he poured hot water over tea bags. He sat at the dining room table with me while the tea brewed. "Looked like you wanted to kill the kid."

"I think Marlena was right about Blake," I said. "I think he's beyond repair."

"What are you talking about?" Kyle said. "He was at your hospital bed the whole time and wouldn't leave until he knew you were going to be okay."

"It was only because he knew he was responsible," I said. "Get the tea and we'll talk."

"You're scaring me, Malcolm," Kyle said as he brought the tea set to the table.

I squeezed a little honey into my cup and stirred.

"My nephew has been doing gay porn since he got to L.A.," I said. "He doesn't know I know it yet."

"What?" Kyle asked. "Get out."

"Hamilton James is behind all of this," I said. "He's got Deacon working for him starring in videos and that's how *our* private videos got leaked. Had to be. He's got a whole lot of young men working porn for him, including DeMarco's man Compton, and now my nephew."

"That's crazy."

"And I'm pretty sure Hamilton was behind my getting beat up in East Hollywood," I said. "I think Lamont Murphy is in on it too. I'd know the man's voice anywhere."

"Wait, hold up. Explain."

I updated Kyle on everything I remembered but pretended not to. The invitation. Thinking I was summoned by Tyrell. Hamilton's revelation. My deal to call off the LADS guys and keep quiet in exchange for Hamilton not releasing Blake's videos.

"I never should have made that deal," I said. "Hamilton's crazy. The boycott was obviously working."

"Well, I never got to tell you how well it was working," Kyle said. "You went off and got yourself beat up while I was in Vegas. The gospel single never took off—a flop. And he lost his billing on a very lucrative old-school tour planned for the holiday season."

It was exciting to learn we'd made a bit of a difference in Tommie Jordan's career.

"Of course, now that I lived…what if Hamilton decides to go after me again?"

"He won't if he's smart," Kyle said. "He knows there's too much attention on you because of the loose association with Tommie and Tyrell. He won't want any more of those associations coming to light, and he certainly doesn't want any more hits to their checkbooks."

"You think?"

"Girl, please," Kyle said and started laughing. "If anything, you need to go out there and get your man, Tyrell, and get LADS back. You wouldn't advise DeMarco and them to sit back, would you?"

"Of course not," I said. But making empowered decisions often came when the odds looked in your favor, not when you were being blackmailed into doing something you didn't want.

"Because you're forgetting two things, Malcolm," Kyle said. "One, you've got Tommie and Hamilton on tape revealing everything about Tommie's undercover life."

"True."

"And two, I didn't make a deal with Hamilton," Kyle said. "I've got your back."

CHAPTER 36

Before reaching out to Tyrell Kincaid, I needed to clear the air with my nephew. I was the grown adult and knew, after my talk with Kyle, that sitting back like a long-suffering heroine wasn't the way to teach Blake what he needed to learn this summer.

I opened the guest room door—no warning—and saw Blake lying on his back pleasuring himself while half keeping an eye on the computer screen next to him.

"Get out here in the living room," I said. "*Now*, Blake."

"Oh shit," Blake said and sat up, his thing still at high noon outside the elastic of his basketball shorts. "Unc, don't I get no privacy?"

"Get decent and get out here. Two minutes."

I was firm, but not angry, as I didn't want to erupt into a shouting match with my nephew. That was Marlena's way of dealing with her problems with Blake. Still, I needed him to know that I meant business.

"What's so important that you couldn't wait for me to handle my business?" Blake asked when he emerged from the guest room. His basketball shorts had been exchanged for jeans, and he was shirtless.

"Sit down, mister," I said and pointed to the exact spot I wanted him to be. "First, you're nineteen, you own no property and have no money, so you do as you're told…especially when you're in my place."

Blake rolled his eyes and head around, in one of those I've-heard-this-before reactions.

"So what happened? You talked to my mom again? She tell you something else I did wrong back in Indiana?"

It would be so easy to send you *back* to Indiana, I thought.

"Actually, this is about what you've been doing wrong since you moved to L.A."

"I ain't been up to nothing," Blake said and got up in that guilty-but-pretending-to-be-innocent mode of youthful pleading. "I been stuck in this house, if anything, bored out my mind."

"But you'd say it's better than being stuck in the house in Indiana, wouldn't you?" I asked. "Because your mom and I can easily arrange for you to go back like yesterday if you want."

Blake started walking toward the guest room.

"Make one more step and I'm telling your mom about the porn and about how you've been making a few dollars on the side with Hamilton James."

He stopped and turned back to me.

"Huh?"

"I know what you've been doing here in L.A.," I said.

"What are you talking about?"

"I don't know how you've been sneaking out to do this, or how you got hooked up with Hamilton James and his porn circuit, but it's going to stop today."

"How do you know this?"

"I talked to Hamilton directly," I said. "I saw you on the screen acting like a whore in heat."

"Well, I don't see how that's any different than those

videos you made with your ex," Blake said, as if he had something on me.

"Those were private videos and I didn't get paid for them."

"Blah, blah, blah. It's the same old story. You didn't consent. You didn't get paid. You were in a relationship," Blake said. "Tell me what's worse? Gettin' paid, or being a ho for nothing."

Don't engage him, Malcolm. But it might be time to pull a Marlena.

"WHY DON'T YOU ASK YOUR MOTHER?" I said and pulled out my cell phone. "Marlena would love to know that you have proven her right. That you're a LOSER LIKE YOUR DADDY with no plans and no future."

I hated pulling the like-your-daddy card with Blake. I knew, based on my conversations with Marlena, that Blake had issues when it came to his father not being around most of his life. Marlena's and my father was the closest thing Blake had to a father figure while growing up. I was that figure now.

"That is not true," Blake said and sat down. I couldn't tell if this was an act or an effort to tone down our discussion before it escalated. "I am not a loser. Don't tell her. I don't want to go back to Indiana, Unc."

"Really? Because you're going to have to man up and prove you want…you *deserve* to stay here in L.A."

"I want to stay," Blake said. "I can't help it that I'm young and I have needs…sex, money, fame, you know. I know you know. You were nineteen once."

I knew quite well what nineteen was like when you're young, Black, and gay. Kyle and I had done our own share of damage and potentially damaging scenarios back in the day. The difference between Blake and me was that I was in college and focused on things in addition to being young, Black, and gay. Like studying. Doing student government. Celebrating at dorm room birthday parties. We were still too early in the tech age to have ready access to computers, the ability to make our own videos or to meet online strangers who were not looking out for our best interests.

"I'm not going to fall for the shared life experiences line," I said. "But I will let you in on something before we continue. It's only fair."

"What?"

"I believe Hamilton James and Lamont Murphy ordered those men to beat me up," I said. "I can't prove it, but it's just a hunch. Hamilton probably didn't trust me as much as I didn't trust him, so after he and I agreed to keep silent about our respective secrets, he arranged to keep me silent... permanently."

"You saying this is all my fault? That you got beat up?"

"I'm not saying it's your fault," I said. "I'm just saying if you don't shape up soon, going back to Indiana *will* be your fault."

CHAPTER 37

Tyrell hadn't been around for a few weeks, but I knew that I wanted to see him. Mainly to make sure he had emerged unscathed from his recent tabloid follies. Somehow, the social-worker-as-romantic was emerging, and that was a side of my personality I knew was dangerous. Led me to feel sorry for and date men like Deacon. And the few before him.

After all, it was being linked to Tyrell and Tommie's scandal that had brought on weeks of public scrutiny by the paparazzi as well as isolation in my apartment. If anything, it should have been Tyrell reaching out to me. Along with Deacon. Along with Lamont Murphy.

The funny thing, though, is once your mind puts something out into the universe, the universe delivers.

Later that evening, just as I was looking to find a contact number for Tyrell, there was a knock at the front door.

Tyrell was there looking for me.

CHAPTER 38

I wouldn't be surprised or upset if you didn't invite me in," Tyrell said.

He had a blank look on his face as he stood outside my screen door. Nothing about Tyrell had changed over the past few weeks. He looked like he'd had his regular share of meals and fitness, and I knew that celebrity isolation was nothing like regular-people isolation. In the event there were still photographers lurking around or following him, I opened the door to let him in. Quickly.

"I was just thinking about you," I said, not wanting to sound overly excited or eager. I was just being honest. I had a list of questions and explanations I wanted to seek, but since I wasn't a partner, boyfriend, or even romantic consideration as far as I was concerned, I decided to slow down and let Tyrell say what he came to say.

"That's good to hear. I've been thinking about you a lot." He took off his athletic jacket and placed it near the spot he'd taken on my sofa weeks earlier. "Mind if I sit?"

"Please do," I said. I was leery if his quiet kindness was authentically Tyrell, as before, or if it was a calm before something stormy. We sat in silence for a few seconds. "So what's up?"

If this was to be some type of atonement session, I would leave it up to him to do the atoning. I had done nothing wrong in our delicate friendship, acquaintanceship, dancing around attraction, so I didn't think I should go first in conversation.

"I feel like I let you down these past weeks," Tyrell said. "I heard about your attack. I feel bad about that."

I wondered how he heard. That part of the story the gossip bloggers didn't follow up on. Too much reality, not enough sex or fantasy, I'm sure. Didn't even make a blurb in the *L.A. Times* or even the *L.A. Sentinel*, the Black-owned newspaper in the city.

"It happened and it was awful," I said. I shared with him the details I could remember of being kicked and punched; the meeting prior at The Standard. "They left me for dead. Not cute. But I'm here."

He reached out his arms. Caressed my face, where I was still tender and healing from the beating. I winced with his touch.

"Come here, Malcolm," he said and pulled me to him. "I'm so sorry, Malcolm. I'm sorry I wasn't there for you."

I felt comforted in his arms, much, I'm sure, the same way he'd felt when he stretched out across my sofa and lap after Tommie's initial sex club scandal weeks earlier.

"There really wasn't anything you could have done," I said. "Unless you knew it was Hamilton who invited me to The Standard?"

"Hamilton? Tommie's manager? I'm not, and wasn't, in on anything they've worked up."

"It's crazy," I said and pulled away from Tyrell. Walked across the room. "I thought it was you inviting me over for...I don't know, a romantic gesture, a date. I don't know. I was stupid, head in the clouds."

I explained how Hamilton asked me to call off the LADS

activism or else he'd release the videos Blake had made since arriving in L.A.

"He said that I was messing up yours, his, and Tommie's careers with the boycotts," I said, after explaining our grassroots efforts to bring down Tommie Jordan. I wondered if I was telling him too much or if he already knew all this. "He even said you and Tommie got married in Massachusetts. I don't know if that part was true or just a lie to try and keep us apart?"

"We're *not* married," Tyrell said, and rolled his eyes. "Trust me on that. I wouldn't be that dumb to marry a serial cheater."

"Thank God," I said.

"Now I feel really bad," Tyrell said. He walked over to me from the sofa. "Tommie and I are the reason you…"

"There's no blame, Tyrell," I said. "I had X-rated videos all over the Internet. I mean, which came first, the chicken or the egg? It's a hairflip now."

He chuckled. "Still, I feel like I let you down," he said. "You're not the kind of guy my dad would want me to let down. You know that's what made me like you, right?"

He was rambling and I wasn't getting it.

"You're not making any sense, Tyrell."

"I'm nervous," he said. "It was how you talked about your dad, and how he influenced you, and how you were doing LADS to raise those young boys who didn't have what we were lucky enough to have…"

"Father figures," I said, completing Tyrell's thought and sentence.

I knew Tyrell had lost his father in recent years, which connected us. People of any age, whether they are kids or grown adults, who have lost a parent have a special, and unspoken, bond that only *they* can understand with each other.

In our initial meeting Tyrell talked about how important his father was, especially when he was first dealing with his sexual orientation in high school in D.C. That supportive, open-door policy with his father was what Tyrell said helped him through his UCLA years, keeping up an image as a college basketball player, and being in an undercover relationship with Tommie—especially during Tommie's first *known* affair with some guy named Rafael Dominguez, and even more so during an HIV scare when they all thought they were affected due to Tommie's flings with Rafael.

"Right," Tyrell said. "When I heard you talk about how you were raised and how that influenced you to be the person you are...and now you're doing the same with young men who are not your own. That was the moment I knew."

Tyrell was smiling and our eyes locked on each others. I knew too. I didn't want to say it first, though, so I waited a beat for him to continue.

"That was the moment I think I fell in love with you, Malcolm."

I didn't want to deflate the moment with any questions or doubts about myself or the feelings Tyrell said he had for me. So I nodded and smiled back.

"I take that as a..." he asked.

I paused for a moment, ready to go where it was easy for me—my head. But my heart felt something else.

"Yes," I said. "I agree. I don't think I love you, but I definitely *like* you. I like you a lot, Tyrell."

Tyrell leaned down toward me. Kissed my forehead. Stared into my eyes.

"That's a start and it sounds good to me, Malcolm," he said. "So where do we go from here?"

I was willing to relinquish complete direction to Tyrell, wanted him to tell *me* what he wanted.

"Where would you *like* to go?" I said. I imagined myself a nineteen- or twenty-year-old Northwestern University student again, a member of the fictitious PBC—Power Bottom Crew—with Kyle and me as its only members, seducing an innocent or not-so-innocent dorm mate.

"Don't ask me a question you don't want the answer to," he said and grinned. Pulled me into him. "Because I'll tell you exactly what I want, Mr. Malcolm."

"I wouldn't have asked," I said back and looked in his eyes to let him know I meant business, "if I didn't want to know the answer."

Tyrell turned me around, hugged me from behind, kissed me on the back of my neck and ears. He pointed in the direction of my bedroom, which was a lucky guess, considering Tyrell hadn't made it past the living room in his only other visit to my apartment.

"You mind?" Tyrell asked and continued kissing me on the ears, neck, back of my head.

My condom and lube stash were pleasantly stocked due to months of no use—safe sex was a must, even with a supposed famous person. My nephew had been in his room most of the evening, happily occupied with his electronica. I was free, smart, and sexually empowered. I knew that after all he'd been through with Tommie Jordan in the past weeks, their relationship had to be over. I wasn't up for relationship triangle drama, especially starting something with someone already in a relationship. That would be so un-LADS-like.

But I was definitely ready to experience what Tyrell had to offer in the more-than-friends department.

So I answered, without hesitating, "No, I don't mind."

CHAPTER 39

An hour after we made love Tyrell and I lay across my bed in a hot, sweaty daze.

I tried getting all thoughts of Tyrell being a celebrity out of my mind, and seeing him as just Tyrell. But who was I kidding? He was Tyrell Kincaid, a pro baller with *all that*, and it was better than any magazine or video. His body, a complete dream. Mine, not a complete dream. But who cared? He smacked, flipped, rubbed down so well, and so thoughtfully, that we both managed to finish at the same exact time. Unbelievably in sync.

We stared at each other, Tyrell on his back, me stretched across his chest. His legs scrunched so they wouldn't dangle over the end of my queen-sized mattress. Our hands and fingers tracing the other's. The candle light flickering and magnifying our shadows against the wall. El DeBarge crooning on the iPod speakers about being loved in a special way. It felt intimate. Felt right.

Even though we exchanged very few words, it wasn't because of any post-sex weirdness that often came with the immature relationships of my twenties. I knew Tyrell and I had a very special bond. Words weren't needed. So we touched. Stared. Smiled. Wondered.

In the middle of the night, long into Tyrell's deep sleep and soft snoring, I crept out of my bedroom and into the living room with my cell phone. I wasn't one to gossip, but I knew my best friend would appreciate knowing that his prediction was coming true.

That Tyrell and I were well on our way to becoming something more than friends.

CHAPTER 40

Tyrell stayed all night. I was relieved. It was a sign, I hoped, that he didn't view me as another groupie—as Diana Ross sang about—to be touched in the morning and then just walked away from. After all I'd tried teaching the LADS guys about self-respect and relationships, the last thing I wanted to do was contradict my words.

In the morning Tyrell was all smiles as he ate the scrambled eggs, cheese grits, turkey sausage, and coffee I'd prepared. Something about making food for a man the morning after makes you feel all official, even if you're still unsure about the road ahead.

"If this is what being with an Indiana man is all about," he said, with a grin and a swallow, "then I know I'm about to be the fattest ex-ball player around."

"I don't cook like this every day," I said and massaged his shoulders. Felt a little too Destiny's Child "Cater 2 U," but that type of catering to a man was definitely warranted after the first night together. And oh, what a night it was. "Only for special occasions like this. And when I watch *The Neelys* on Food Network."

"Come here," he said and pulled me to sit on his lap. "There better be a second, third, fourth, and thousandth time like last night, Malcolm."

"Only if I get to enjoy this some more," I said and squirmed in his lap until he came to life down there again.

We kissed. Kept it tasteful and PG-13, in case my nephew walked in ready for breakfast. I felt like a teenager, so full of the feelings that came with a brand-new relationship.

"Love my Malcolm," Tyrell said. "Knew it the moment I met you at LADS."

"Stop it," I said. The idea of a professional ball player liking me, or loving me, was unbelievable still. I mean, he was sitting in my tiny kitchen eating breakfast. "Okay. I'm feeling you too."

And then, as if he were reading my mind, he said, "You don't have to worry about Tommie and me. We're over and there's no involvement. Well, except for his niece Keesha, but she's off in boarding school in New England, which I'm paying for. More about that later."

I wouldn't and couldn't say that I loved him, because I didn't. Not yet. Not while there was still unfinished business with Hamilton James, Lamont Murphy, and LADS. Not that they had anything to do with my feelings. I just wanted to resolve them, have a clean slate, then worry about what the future held with Tyrell Kincaid.

"The let's keep it without a label," I said. "If that's okay with you?"

"So I can't call you my man?" Tyrell asked. "I'd be proud to show you off."

"Thanks," I said and looked at his fingers. "But don't you want one of those championship rings one day? There's no way you'll have a career as an out, gay, and Black basketball player."

"I don't care about the ring," he said. "I have a degree. I can do something other than ball. But I might have only one shot with you...and finally having a fulfilling, no-drama life."

I didn't want Tyrell to feel like he had to choose between me or his career in sports, and I told him so.

"Let's give you some time to think," I said and kissed him. "Besides, I have some loose ends to tie up too. No labels and we'll take it from there. Agreed?"

"Absolutely," he said and kissed me again. "Absolutely yes."

CHAPTER 41

Two days later, Bernard wanted an occasion to cook for a large crowd. So I invited the LADS guys over to my apartment for another dinner party and group meeting. Anytime there was free food, you could bet DeMarco, Sergio, and friends would arrive on time. Early, in fact. If I was going to tie up loose ends with Lamont Murphy and LADS, I would need to know the guys had my back.

For this feast, Bernard chose a simple soul theme—oven fried chicken, greens seasoned with apple cider vinegar and jalapeño peppers, Jiffy corn muffins, berry-infused seltzer water, and an ice cream sandwich casserole. Simple, by Bernard's standards. Delicious by everyone else's.

"So what's up with you and Compton," I heard Blake ask DeMarco from his corner of the living room. "I heard you had a little Rihanna moment."

"Oh, Compton," I heard DeMarco commanding attention in a corner of the living room. "I made him kick rocks after he put his hands on me. Sent his ass to jail for two weeks. Blocked his number."

"Mmm-hmm," Blake said. "That's all the story?"

"Ain't no muthafucker gonna play me and then try to make me do porn for coins," DeMarco continued. "And it's literally coins, right, Blake?"

"I don't wanna talk about it," Blake replied from across the room. He was learning, slowly, not to bite just because someone baited him with controversial conversation. "Eat your dinner."

"Don't pay him no mind," Sergio said from another corner of the room. "Y'all need to quit signifying."

"Signifying?" I said. I hadn't heard anyone use that word since my parents' and grandparents' days, used primarily when someone was teasing another in a loving way. Others called it playing the dozens. I was surprised someone born in the '90s knew how to use the word. "You sounding old-school, Sergio."

"Well, I got a little old-school in me," Sergio said. "I'm dating an older man of twenty-five. Haaaaay."

"Which means we're ready for the nursing home in our late thirties," Kyle said and laughed as he peeked into the living room from the kitchen. "But let me tell y'all young girls something…life is much better in your thirties. You got a little cash, a little stability, and a whole lot more confidence."

As the joking and getting reacquainted continued, Bernard brought out bowls of his ice cream sandwich casserole and cups of coffee for the LADS. We were stuffed beyond our belts from dinner, a good sign that Bernard's culinary skills hit the mark again. But no one wanted to pass up dessert. In these times, if it's free and offered, you eat it.

I decided to use the post-dinner lull to address the group and to check in. I had questions. I'm sure they did too. Mainly, I wanted to let them know how proud I was of their efforts to stay together during the reign of Lamont Murphy.

"The blogging and boycotts worked," I said and made sure I looked each of the guys in the eye. "Your willingness to do something on behalf of LADS and the media representations of Black, gay men is something to be commended. You're all young activists and you didn't even know it."

Hand claps, whistles, a few high fives and fist bumps circled the room.

"Well anything for you, Malcolm," DeMarco said. "Because the sooner we can get Lamont Murphy and his tired, nineteen seventies ass out of LADS...ooooh, don't get me started."

DeMarco punched his fist into his other open hand.

"I know," I said. "It's different. But one day we'll have another space. I'm fine with my living room being the space for now."

"Me too," Sergio said from his corner of the room. "Y'all my sistas and I love y'all as much as y'all get on my nerves."

Blake moved to the center of the circle.

"I just wanna thank you for supporting my uncle Malcolm," he said. He started with his head down, but soon looked up and around the circle. "I haven't been the best nephew. Some of y'all know what I'm talking about."

"Mmm-hmm," Sergio whispered and moved his neck. "Some of us seen it too, but no tea, no shade."

"Yeah, please shut up, Sergio," DeMarco said.

"I admit I got mixed up with that easy money they offered a lot of y'all too," Blake said. "Thinking that I'd be a star making porn for Deacon, Compton, and Reverend Murphy. I'm sorry, Uncle Malcolm. I'm sorry for embarrassing you and your work."

"I still can't believe that one," DeMarco said. "Lamont Murphy? The church man? Directing gay porn. Lawwwwd."

I could see a conversation digression and needed to focus. I hugged Blake and continued with the group discussion.

"We're going to get LADS back," I said. "You don't know

this, but your blogs worked. People are starting to pay attention. Some of the fans who liked Tommie Jordan are boycotting him. You don't even hear him on the radio anymore."

"Amen," DeMarco said. "I'll never download a ToJo song again. Or ones that he sings hooks on again. But that won't get you LADS back."

True, declining record sales wouldn't do anything for my work at LADS, though I'm sure it put pressure on Tommie and Hamilton…and their checkbooks. I'm sure they were scrambling for Plans B, C, and D. Much like we were.

"Maybe the thing with Tommie is too big-picture," Kyle said as he and Bernard emerged from the kitchen. "Let's focus on Lamont Murphy. Now, other than Blake, who here saw him in his role of video director?"

No one admitted personal involvement with Lamont, Hamilton, or the videos beyond my nephew.

"So other than Blake's word, we've got nothing to prove Lamont's been less than holy?" Sergio asked. "No proof, no case. And that means no LADS, huh?"

"Who said *we* have to prove anything?" Blake said. "Why not let Lamont prove it *himself*?"

CHAPTER 42

I was confident of my next steps. At least I thought I was.
I knew Kyle had my back. Blake assured me that I could
be a master of technology and quipped this could be done even
at my age. Tyrell let me know that no matter the outcome, with
his support I could start an organization that was ten times
larger than LADS. I didn't want to rely on Tyrell's money
or name to get a new organization started, but I definitely
appreciated his willingness to support. Such a big difference
from Deacon when I wanted to start LADS.

With nothing to worry about, nothing to lose, and new love
on my side, I called Lamont Murphy and asked to schedule a
meeting with him at LADS. He agreed.

CHAPTER 43

L amont Murphy smirked as he opened the door to let me in. It was after business hours, but I'd made an appointment so he couldn't back out.

"You wanted to talk about what, Malcolm?" he asked. "Transition?"

"Yeah," I said. "Even though your style and focus is different, I still care about LADS. I just wanted to check in and see how things are with the guys. See if you needed or wanted any information that might help with your new vision for LADS."

Honey, not vinegar, Malcolm.

"Come on in," he said. "We'll meet in your...I mean *my* office."

Lamont Murphy operated with vinegar.

At this point I didn't mind. Our office was where I'd hoped he would take me anyway. Perfect, if this plan was to work.

I followed the reverend and his old-school cologne through the hall and back to the executive director office. I cringed seeing Lamont Murphy's name on the door, as if he were the one responsible for the legacy of success I'd left behind at LADS.

He offered me bottled water, which I declined politely. This wasn't a social call. The nerve of him to try and display manners like his partner-in-crime Hamilton James. Didn't matter. I just needed to remember the instructions Blake told me, including the first step—placing my bag on Lamont's desk—and the rest would fall into place.

"I still keep in touch with some of the guys," I started out. "They say it's different around here. Not bad different…just different."

"Of course," he said. He sat and plopped his shiny purple shoes onto the desktop. If this was his everyday wear, I wondered what colors he'd sport for Easter next spring. "New leadership makes a difference."

I'd let that one slide. Lamont's critique of my leadership style was the last thing on my mind.

"How's DeMarco working out as your front desk person?"

"Slow, unprofessional, always on the computer," Lamont said. He sighed and continued after a beat. "And why is he so damn girly? How did you let him be the face of your organization acting like that? And those damn sunglasses…"

"I never had a problem with DeMarco's demeanor," I said. "He was a growing professional, but if you took time to know his story you'd see just how far he's come. You know he used to turn tricks and do hook-ups with older men to make ends meet, so this job is quite a turnaround."

"If you say so," Lamont said, and adjusted his necktie. "Still a sinner. See, that's what I'm trying to lead these young men to do. Turn their lives over to something more positive and productive, and away from their past sins."

"If that's what you call it," I said. "You know, some would argue that it's that type of…stance…that leads young men like the LADS to not talk to their families, not demand safe sex, live secret lives."

"One would argue," he said. "But not me."

"Point taken," I said. Didn't want to agitate Lamont

Murphy so much that he'd kick me out. Being in his office was the point of this meeting. "Anyway, let's get back to the subject at hand."

"So what about the transition did you want to talk about?" He picked up his cell phone and began toying with the screen, as if he had another pressing engagement that I was keeping him from. "As far as I can tell, it's been smooth. The guys don't even ask about you. We're doing some new things here...new approaches."

"Oh yeah," I said. I hated engaging in small talk. But honey, not vinegar. "Tell me about your new initiatives."

"Well, we've got some great counselors trained in man-aversion techniques," he said and smiled. He seemed proud. Man-aversion techniques. I was sickened. "We're integrating the groups with more young ladies to help the young men see their options. Eventually some attraction is going to happen. Going on some outdoor and sporting trips...summer is winding down, you know. We're gonna help turn these girls into men."

Yeah right, with your purple sweater and black slacks. It's summer all right, I thought.

"Sounds good," I said. But I didn't want to hear any more. The guys had shielded me from all those details of the changes at LADS, which would have made me angrier a lot sooner. "Well, as for my transition. If you don't mind, I need to retrieve my résumé from the computer...I can email it to myself if you don't want me sticking my flash drive in...viruses."

Lamont stood up and put his arm out, welcoming me to his side of the desk. He lingered a little longer than I wanted as I passed in front of him, all part of Lamont's approach, I imagined, with the young men he directed in gay porn.

I sat in Lamont's chair, but he didn't go very far. He stood behind me...immediately behind me. I could feel his—gross—crotch easing toward my shoulder, I hoped by accident.

"This will only take a few minutes," I said and pulled out the device Blake gave me. "I'm not the best with technology, so I apologize if this takes too long."

"Take your time, Malcolm."

I fumbled around some more until the blue light started flickering on the device. Exactly as Blake told me it would. I felt good about what was about to happen. Still, I had to stall just a few minutes.

"So I want to go back to DeMarco for a minute," I said and turned around fast. It was deliberate that I wanted my face in his crotch so that Lamont would feel nervous enough to back away and get in line with my bag on the desk. Like clockwork, he moved and sat where I'd been a few minutes earlier. "I heard a rumor about a second job he took."

"Really? I don't know much about what the staff does outside of work hours. I don't get into their business if it's not LADS related."

"I bet you don't," I said. "But I know you've met my nephew, Blake."

"Blake...hmm, doesn't ring a bell," Lamont said. "He come by LADS?"

"I don't know," I said. "Tell me if you recognize his voice."

I turned up the volume of Lamont's computer. The sounds of Compton, Deacon, and Blake were disgusting for me to listen to again, but caught the interest of Lamont, especially when he heard his voice barking orders of new positions and movements in the background of the uncut video. He jumped up from his seat.

"What the hell are you listening to on my computer?" Lamont asked. "This isn't that kind of organization... anymore. How did you get that?"

"Lamont, I wouldn't do anything crazy if I were you," I said. "You're on camera right now. Just sit back and listen to your work in action."

He looked confused, but continued with his rant.

"I don't believe you, you little Black faggot. How dare you come up into my workplace and denigrate it with these immoral accusations."

"Immoral?" I asked. "How about what you're doing to the boys you're supposedly trying to help? Gay porn and young Black men?"

"What are you talking about?" Lamont asked. "I can see why we fired you from LADS."

"I figured it all out," I said. "You're using your access to the guys at LADS, and probably the so-called ex-gays at your church, to make porn…which you're using to fund the Family First campaign."

He stared at me. Speechless. So I continued.

"Not bad for a little Black faggot, huh?" I asked. "What about your church? Where your grandfather and father used to preach. What are *they* going to think about your involvements and immoral behavior with the little Black faggots, Reverend Lamont Murphy?"

"They're not going to think anything," a voice boomed from the hallway.

Lamont and I turned to see Hamilton James standing in the doorway with a gun in his hand, pointed in my direction.

This was priceless. And scary. My father used to say never to mess with a Black person's pocketbook, or else there'd be trouble. He was right. Except in this case, there were two men's pocketbooks, a network of mega-churches and ministers, along with the whole Family First anti-gay legislation machine.

"You're as smart as they all said, Mr. Malcolm," Hamilton

said as he walked into the room, faux British accent ablaze again. "I wondered how long it would take for you to piece this all together. So now what?"

"Hamilton," Lamont said and tried to motion to his co-conspirator in the direction of the desk and the camera in my bag. Hamilton was focused only on his plan, which was quickly unraveling. As far as I was concerned, it had unraveled, and it would be a matter of minutes before he knew how far gone and done he was.

"Shut up, Lamont," Hamilton said, gun still aimed at me. "You are such a loser for a middleman. Can't even keep a few little Black faggots under control."

"Those little Black faggots can't be controlled," I said. "We're too smart…and we're not gonna take it anymore from people like you, Hamilton, who force celebrities not to be themselves, or you, Lamont, who use your church and position to keep people silent and hurting."

"And what exactly are you gonna do now, Mr. Malcolm?" Hamilton said. "I've got the gun. And remember Sunset Boulevard? I got those guys back to make sure you don't live to tell whatever it is you *think* you know."

"So you were behind my gay-bashing too?" I asked. "Perfect. Just perfect. All this for Tommie Jordan and a few dollars. Perfect."

"That mouth of yours," Hamilton said and moved closer to me. "Before I have you taken care of, why don't you use that mouth to take care of me and Lamont. Show us what you got, like you did in those GayClick videos with our little Deacon."

The idea of performing *that* on Hamilton or vintage-dressing Lamont made me sick. A click and his gun pointed to my head made me assume the position on my knees. One hand on zipper. A tug. A quick adjustment to pull them out of boxer briefs. My face moved closer. My eyes closed. My mouth open.

Then.

A brick flew through the window of Lamont's office, which unhooked the curtains from the valance and brackets. Thank God.

Soon after the brick we heard one car horn, then another in the parking lot behind LADS. Then, chanting picketers showed up with signs featuring pictures of Lamont Murphy, Hamilton James, and Tommie Jordan, and slogans describing just how dangerous the men were to the Black gay community.

"What the fuck?" Hamilton asked and zipped up his suit pants as he looked outside the window. "Shit, I'm ruined. What's with all those people out there?"

When television news trucks from the local stations showed up minutes later, I knew that Blake was onto something when he schooled me on the merits of flash mobs, political art, and the power of the Internet. All this from someone who seemed only to concern himself with becoming a rapper and the next piece for whoever paid.

"Fuck," Lamont said. "Why are you doing this to LADS? What are you doing to your father's legacy?"

Now he was concerned with legacy and image.

"What about *your* father's legacy?" I asked. "You ruined yours the moment you started doing business with Hamilton James and Tommie Jordan."

I pulled on my bag and Blake's camera fell out on the table. Lamont looked at it as if it were a weapon.

"You were recording this conversation?" Hamilton asked and reached for the camera. "This is unauthorized, Malcolm. I'll sue you for all your Silver Lake–living ass has. I'll keep you tied up in court for years."

"I just want you to know this is going out live on the Internet as we speak, so I wouldn't make any threats or try to harm me, unless you want to add murder to your list of crimes," I said. "Oh, and how's this for an encore?"

I pressed another button on Lamont's computer. The video Blake had shot on his first day in L.A., when we were the invisible and unimportant witnesses to Tommie and Hamilton's post-sex club intervention, with Tommie outing himself and his secret gay life, streamed across the screen, and again, thanks to Blake, was making its debut on the Internet. The whole private conversation broadcast for the public record. So much for that interview on *The Black Morning Radio Show*. The world would now know Tommie Jordan was a liar.

"You're no better than the white man out there trying to lynch a brotha," Hamilton said. "This is what you're teaching in LADS. Gay shit over uplifting the race?"

I thought about responding, but left it alone.

Lamont chimed in, his head in his hands, as he realized his mega-church kingdom and family legacy was crumbling.

"Lord, please help me," Lamont said. "I'm a married man with kids. I ain't done nothing wrong but try to give some young Black men opportunities to make a little extra cash. I didn't put a gun to their heads and make 'em do nothing."

"Lamont, the money is the gun," I said. "And as for white men bringing down Black men…I'll give you that argument on a structural and systematic level. But just take a look in the mirror or the camera. Ain't nobody in this room white."

CHAPTER 44

An amazing thing happened that evening.

After the eleven o'clock news, the remaining members of the LADS Board of Directors held an emergency meeting that lasted until almost two in the morning. I got my job and my organization back. It took some debate, apparently, because I was still considered tainted goods due to those Deacon videos on GayClick. But my overall work record and contributions to LADS prevailed.

And then the next two weeks. The issues of Black gay men made local and national headlines in legitimate news sources and the credible blogosphere, as well as the titillating gossip sites. Of course, all sources looked at the story of Tommie Jordan, his agent Hamilton Jones, and the Reverend Lamont Murphy through different lenses.

To some, the three men symbolized the polarizing opinions keeping their constituents locked in a closet of denial. To some, they represented victims—more Black men being brought down by the so-called white man's evil (i.e., homosexuality). To others, they represented an opportunity to speculate about who else within Black celebrity lived similar stories, and they pursued these with a vengeance. Livonia Birmingham, successful gossip columnist that she was, put it bluntly in her call for more outings—and sought all the jaded exes of gay closeted celebrities to come forward. As she put it in her TV show promos immediately after the Lamont, Tommie, Hamilton blowup, "For every closeted gay celebrity, there's a bitter ex whose been told to shut up. I wanna hear you speak!"

So when I received an invitation to *The Livonia Birmingham Show* in New York City, it confused me. I was scared, to say the least. Kyle flew with me, acting as my agent and attorney, as we negotiated what the interview would focus on.

I'd seen Livonia Birmingham skewer celebrities for anything she found annoying, even in the middle of the live interview segments. Plus, her flair for the dramatic and an unpredictable personality—anyone would be scared, even with the prospect of reaching ten million viewers. I didn't want her going off on me for, as she billed it in the promos, "Bringing down the house of Tommie Jordan and the most powerful Black agent in Hollywood, Hamilton James."

But she didn't. Blame it on my naivety.

"Livonia, I'm a little mad at you for not having me on earlier," I said and chuckled before she even got to introduce me in her scripted monologue about me and my work.

The audience hushed. Ready for a famous Livonia Birmingham rampage.

"Huh?!? What did you just say?" She flicked a piece of her honey-blond hair out of her face. "This is the *Livonia Birmingham Show*, not *Malcolm 'the do-gooder' Campbell Show*."

"I wish you'd had me on earlier," I said. "I could have given you the scoop long before anyone else, girl. I had the original footage…but I wanted you to have the exclusive, because I love you so much."

"Oh," she said and flicked more hair around her shoulders.

"Because I love you too. You're about to blow up, Mr. Malcolm. You brought down Hamilton James. I hope you have an agent for all the good things coming your way."

"Thanks," I said and smiled. Relieved that she didn't read me on national television.

"You're lucky you're so cute today," she said, "because I was this close to pulling a Livonia on you."

And I don't know what came over me...the cameras, the audience's laughter, the adrenaline and nerves, or just the confidence in knowing that underneath the hair, big boobs, and mean-hearted gossip, Livonia was just another person. So I replied, "Livonia, girl, I ain't scared of you. You haven't seen me pull a Malcolm."

The audience loved our interplay and the rest was a coup for me and for LADS.

"Now that we're best friends, Malcolm," Livonia said and moved in closer to me, as if we were longtime gay man and fag hag BFFs, "tell me about that tall glass of chocolate ball player they say you're drinking from."

I didn't tell her about Tyrell and me. Kyle had advised me not to talk about romance yet. Too soon. Besides, I wanted to give Tyrell space to tell his own story in his own time.

I could see the audience members breathe a sigh of relief, some a little saddened, because Livonia and I had a friendly and serious conversation about the state of Black, gay men. She even allowed me to challenge her on why outing people wasn't the best policy, but that we needed her influence to make changes in our communities of color so people wouldn't feel like they had to hide being gay.

"Let's put it this way, Livonia," I said. "Straight women, especially those of color, need to develop a gaydar first of all. Or at least should be comfortable acknowledging there are gay men out there."

"Amen," Livonia replied. "The naïve 'I don't know any gay men' attitude is so 1950s chic."

"You ain't never lied," I said. I felt a little too comfortable onstage and on camera with Livonia Birmingham. "When gay men live in a world where they feel comfortable being themselves, without fear of being judged, they'll feel safe to be out, and won't spring those gay surprises on anyone. Then you straight women won't have to play the guessing games about your potential partners and fiancés. We're all allies in this together, playing that guessing game."

As for the four who played games with my life and career, I cared, but didn't really care, about what happened to Tommie, Hamilton, Deacon, or Lamont.

Three lost their careers. Hamilton, Deacon, and Lamont faced criminal and civil charges, ranging from contributing to the delinquency of minors, to prostitution rings, to money laundering, to attempted murder, to distributing underage porn online, to violating my privacy and unlawful use of images for public use without permission. I pushed the last charge, due to those videos that I made, but didn't *really* make, ending up online because of Deacon. Tommie made yet another comeback, reconciled with his former singing group Renaissance Phoenix, and began touring with other 1990s and 2000s R&B male groups. He remained in the closet, still.

All I cared that I was appointed to lead LADS again. I cared that I would be able to lead the young men and the organization back to the original reason I started it—that being smart, culturally empowered, and sexually empowered led to mental and physical health and well-being.

CHAPTER 45

Tyrell held a press conference soon after my *Livonia Birmingham Show* appearance and told his truth, with my best friend Kyle by his side fielding any legal questions.

Though he mentioned that he and Tommie Jordan had a complicated friendship and business partnership at one point, he said he'd allow Tommie to tell his own truth on his time. On Kyle's advice, and to my relief, Tyrell made no announcement about his newest romantic interest—me. It wasn't needed. I was ready for life out of the spotlight.

The day after his press conference, Tyrell resigned from his contract playing professional basketball. He wouldn't tell me if he was pressured to resign, resigned on his own, or if he was straight-out fired.

But one sign that he didn't *just* resign was the eight-figure check he received from the league immediately after submitting his resignation, along with a contract agreeing never to talk about anyone other than himself when speaking of his career in professional basketball. I guess his former bosses and owners worried that Tyrell would out other gay ball players, thus harming the reputation (in their minds) of the league. In my view, if they were smart, they'd have catered to the gay audience a whole lot more—all those fine, dark, sweaty men running around in basketball shorts always kept the gays talking. There was an audience. A loyal one. Plenty of money to be made, if they marketed right.

"But I'm relieved, so don't press it, Malcolm," Tyrell said as he propped his head on my lap. I rubbed the side of his face. "As long as I got you, I'm cool."

He was as down-to-earth as when we first met, still visiting me at my little Silver Lake apartment. The only difference now was my security guard team watching the apartment building. Death threats from the FCNs—the Fake Christian Nice crew, as I now called them—after what LADS and I "did" to Reverend Lamont Murphy. How about what *they* did to me or the guys at LADS?

"You say that now," I said, and realized again I was doubting Tyrell's attraction to me. I would have to stop that. Tyrell Kincaid, former pro basketball player, was in love with me. "And I hope you say that forever."

"Believe me babe, I will," he said, staring up at me. "And you know what else?"

"I don't know. You tell me."

What more could I want? I was living every gay guy's fantasy by dating a famous athlete. That he was nice, intelligent, and concerned about my dreams and wants was icing on the cake.

"Once you get settled into your LADS work again and I start these speaking engagements all over the place, I want to move us into a nice little house," he said. "Nothing too extravagant, but a place where I know you're safe, babe."

"We won't need security forever," I said. "But yes, I love that you want to keep me safe."

"And then I want to hire Blake and DeMarco to manage my schedule and office," he said. "And if you want your sister Marlena and your mom close, for Blake's sake, I will have a little guest house built on the property behind our house."

"That's all?" I said and smiled. I didn't want to start out our new relationship with him managing all the shots. I still valued being independent, empowered, and in control of my life.

"I'm sorry, Malcolm," Tyrell said. "Those are all my wants. What are yours?"

I leaned down closer to Tyrell's face and kissed him.

"Hiring Blake and DeMarco is fine," I said and smiled. "They will appreciate the opportunity, I'm sure. Blake doesn't want to move back to Indiana after all the excitement he's experienced here in L.A. I don't know about Marlena and my mom living that close to me. We'll talk."

"Good deal," he said. "I'm all for keeping it drama free."

"Well, about the house," I said. I didn't know how to put this without sounding like a gold digger. "It's your money, so make it as extravagant or simple as you want. I happen to like gyms and exercise equipment, now that you've hired us personal trainers, so a home gym would be nice. But I have another request...no, two."

"Whatever you want, Malcolm."

Tyrell was nothing like Deacon, thank God.

But I just wanted to put it out there so there was no mistaking what my don't-cross lines were. Years from now, I would be grateful for having this conversation with Tyrell. Not only would our friendship and romantic relationship continue to thrive, thanks to being open about our likes, dislikes, and what were non-negotiables, but our wedding after the Prop. 8 court decision finally came in would be a dream come true, and a major lesson in negotiating and planning, for both of us and our families. I would agree to sign a pre-nup, not because we anticipated a breakup (which would never come, by the way), but because I didn't feel entitled to anything Tyrell had earned *before* we got together—and he'd earned *a lot*.

After our wedding, we'd see a level of fortune and success beyond our wildest dreams. Our romantic partnership would soon add a business component, the Mal&Ty Group, with my best friend Kyle as chief business officer, which would focus on representing queer people of color entertainers, actors, athletes, musicians, writers, and keynote speakers.

It would also include representing my nephew, Blake, who would eventually succeed as an openly gay, award-winning, multi-platinum hip-hop star and songwriter, including a reality show, which would air on BET and LOGO, winning over the hearts and minds of his generation, which parlayed into work on a national platform with a newly created Presidential Task Force on Queer Youth of Color, and later marrying the love of his life, DeMarco Jennings, my office manager at LADS, who would finish undergraduate degrees in Pan-African Studies and Women's, Gender, and Sexuality Studies at Cal State L.A. and a master's degree in Social Work at University of Southern California, and who I'd eventually groom to lead the next and new generation of LADS coming through the organization on Crenshaw in South L.A.—we'd never forget our roots. Marlena would be proud and eat her words that there was no such thing as a gay rapper, since Blake would find success just as he was, and would eventually make her a grandmother after he and DeMarco utilized technology to have their own biological children via a surrogate.

Indeed, years from now, when Hillary Clinton actually did consider another serious run to become President of the United States (I'd make the Food Network's new star Bernard, Kyle's man—they'd stay together forever—eat his words about my 2008 primary vote for Hillary), and after Barack Obama continued to make history for all the communities that deserved advocacy, I'd look back and realize that the key to Tyrell's and my successful life together was our communication…and also me getting over my nervousness over Tyrell's celebrity status. At the end of the day, he was just another man who loved coming home to his man. Me.

"All right, Tyrell, you asked for it," I said. "One, this mature relationship thing is new territory for me. So let's just play it forward day by day, make each day better than yesterday."

"It's handled, babe."

"Next, leave the computers, laptops, all that jazz in our respective offices. Maybe we can keep our tablets in our room."

"I can handle that," he said. "What else?"

"I know you're eight years younger than me and into all those technology and gadgets," I said. "But I don't want any cameras inside our bedroom. Security cameras outside the house, yes. Inside, not so much. Blame it on being out of touch with my youth."

We laughed.

"Agreed," he said. "That's all?"

"What do you mean, that's all?" I asked. "You see what computers and cameras did to us this summer. And I don't want any repeats of what my ex did to me."

Tyrell cupped my butt in his hands and pulled me into him. I felt excitement coming on down there. Both of us.

"I love it when you're giving orders, boss," Tyrell said and winked. "But I should be worried about you exposing me…I'm the famous one in the relationship."

"Ha, you're funny," I said.

"Just kidding, babe," he said and kissed me. "Can I make another request? Since we're stating our needs and all right now."

"Whatever you want, big daddy," I said.

"Since we're doing away with the computers and cameras in our bedroom, can we keep *doing it* like we're making GayClick videos?"

The magic of membership in the PBC.

"Tyrell, that's a given," I said and gave him the eye that said I was ready to take care of both our needs. "You don't *even* have to worry about that."

About the Author

Originally from Detroit, Michigan, Frederick Smith (FrederickLSmith.com) is a graduate of the University of Missouri School of Journalism and Loyola University Chicago. A finalist for the PEN Center Emerging Voices Fellowship and an alum of the VONA (Voices of Our Nations Arts Foundation) Writers Workshop, Fred is a social justice advocate. He lives in Los Angeles and works with college students to help them find their voices and develop pride in their cultural and gender identities. He is the author of *Down for Whatever* and *Right Side of the Wrong Bed*, a Lambda Literary Award finalist.

Books Available From Bold Strokes Books

Play It Forward by Frederick Smith. When the worlds of a community activist and a pro basketball player collide, little do they know that their dirty little secrets can lead to a public scandal…and an unexpected love affair. (978-1-62639-235-9)

GingerDead Man by Logan Zachary. Paavo Wolfe sells horror but isn't prepared for what he finds in the oven or the bathhouse; he's in hot water again, and the killer is turning up the heat. (978-1-62639-236-6)

Myth and Magic: Queer Fairy Tales, edited by Radclyffe and Stacia Seaman. Myth, magic, and monsters—the stuff of childhood dreams (or nightmares) and adult fantasies. (978-1-62639-225-0)

Blackthorn by Simon Hawk. Rian Blackthorn, Master of the Hall of Swords, vowed he would not give in to the advances of Prince Corin, but he finds himself dueling with more than swords as Corin pursues him with determined passion. (978-1-62639-226-7)

Café Eisenhower by Richard Natale. A grieving young man who travels to Eastern Europe to claim an inheritance finds friendship, romance, and betrayal, as well as a moving document relating a secret lifelong love affair. (978-1-62639-217-5)

Balls & Chain by Eric Andrews-Katz. In protest of the marriage equality bill, the son of Florida's governor has been kidnapped. Agent Buck 98 is back, and the alligators aren't the only things biting. (978-1-62639-218-2)

Murder in the Arts District by Greg Herren. An investigation into a new and possibly shady art gallery in New Orleans' fabled Arts District soon leads Chanse into a dangerous world of forgery, theft…and murder. A Chanse MacLeod mystery. (978-1-62639-206-9)

Rise of the Thing Down Below by Daniel W. Kelly. Nothing kills sex on the beach like a fishman out of water…Third in the Comfort Cove Series. (978-1-62639-207-6)

Calvin's Head by David Swatling. Jason Dekker and his dog, Calvin, are homeless in Amsterdam when they stumble on the victim of a grisly murder—and become targets for the calculating killer, Gadget. (978-1-62639-193-2)

The Return of Jake Slater by Zavo. Jake Slater mistakenly believes his lover, Ben Masters, is dead. Now a wanted man in Abilene, Jake rides to Mexico to begin a new life and heal his broken heart. (978-1-62639-194-9)

Backstrokes by Dylan Madrid. When pianist Crawford Paul meets lifeguard Armando Leon, he accepts Armando's offer to help him overcome his fear of water by way of private lessons. As friendship turns into a summer affair, their lust for one another turns to love. (978-1-62639-069-0)

The Raptures of Time by David Holly. Mack Frost and his friends journey across an alien realm, through homoerotic adventures, suffering humiliation and rapture, making friends and enemies, always seeking a gateway back home to Oregon. (978-1-62639-068-3)

The Thief Taker by William Holden. Unreliable lovers, twisted family secrets, and too many dead bodies wait for Thomas Newton in London—where he soon discovers that all the plotting is aimed directly at him. (978-1-62639-054-6)

Waiting for the Violins by Justine Saracen. After surviving Dunkirk, a scarred and embittered British nurse returns to Nazi-occupied Brussels to join the Resistance, and finds that nothing is fair in love and war. (978-1-62639-046-1)

Turnbull House by Jess Faraday. London 1891: Reformed criminal Ira Adler has a new, respectable life—but will an old flame and the promise of riches tempt him back to London's dark side…and his own? (978-1-60282-987-9)

Stronger Than This by David-Matthew Barnes. A gay man and a lesbian form a beautiful friendship out of grief when their soul mates are tragically killed. (978-1-60282-988-6)

Death Came Calling by Donald Webb. When private investigator Katsuro Tanaka is hired to look into the death of a high profile lawyer, he becomes embroiled in a case of murder and mayhem. (978-1-60282-979-4)

Love in the Shadows by Dylan Madrid. While teaming up to bring a killer to justice, a lustful spark is ignited between an American man living in London and an Italian spy named Luca. (978-1-60282-981-7)

Cutie Pie Must Die by R.W. Clinger. Sexy detectives, a muscled quarterback, and the queerest murders…when murder is most cute. (978-1-60282-961-9)